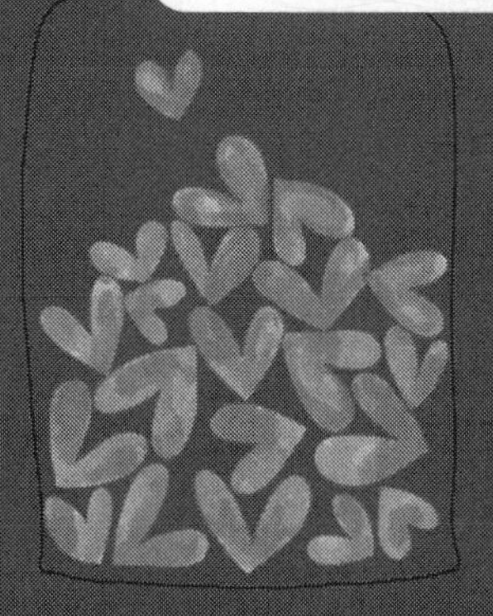

Cover Design: Jay Aheer

Editing done by Jenny Sims Editing4Indies

Proofing Julie Deaton by Deaton Author Services

Proofing by Judy's proofreading

Interior Design by Christina Smith

Books By Natasha Madison

The Only One Series
Only One Kiss
Only One Chance
Only One Night
Only One Touch
Only One Regret
Only One Moment
Only One Love
Only One Forever

Southern Series
Southern Chance
Southern Comfort
Southern Storm
Southern Sunrise
Southern Heart
Southern Heat
Southern Secrets
Southern Sunshine

This Is
This is Crazy
This Is Wild
This Is Love
This Is Forever

Hollywood Royalty
Hollywood Playboy
Hollywood Princess
Hollywood Prince

Something So Series
Something Series
Something So Right
Something So Perfect
Something So Irresistible
Something So Unscripted
Something So BOX SET

Tempt Series
Tempt The Boss
Tempt The Playboy
Tempt The Ex
Tempt The Hookup
Heaven & Hell Series
Hell And Back
Pieces Of Heaven

Love Series
Perfect Love Story
Unexpected Love Story
Broken Love Story

Faux Pas
Mixed Up Love
Until Brandon

Reed

I never wanted to be a cowboy, living in a small town was suffocating.
The military was my out.
I saw every place I ever wanted and everything that nightmares are made of.
Until I almost lost my life and then I ended up back home.

Hazel

Finding out that I was pregnant the night before I left for college changed everything.
I left that small town and vowed to never return.
When my grandfather died, I had no choice but to go back home.
The plan was just for two weeks.
I thought it would be quick and easy, until he was standing at the back door asking questions.
Secrets never stay secrets for long in this town.

Dedication

To you the reader. without you there is no me!
someday when the pages of my life end,
i know that you will be one of the most beautiful
chapters.
anonymous

Southern sunshine

Prologue

Reed

"I CAN'T BELIEVE you're leaving," my little sister, Harlow, says from beside me.

With a laugh, I look over at her. "You already came in and measured my room for your glam room," I remind her, and she rolls her eyes.

"Yeah." She crosses her arms over her chest. "Until Mom found out and started crying about her baby leaving." She shakes her head and fake vomits. I have this sudden twinge in my chest when I think about not being here anymore. "It's annoying. They still have me."

She turns and walks back into the crowd of people. We are at Amelia's bar celebrating Asher becoming a cop and me leaving. "There he is," Quinn says, putting his arm around me to slap my shoulder. He's my older brother, and he followed in my cowboy father's footsteps. It made following in his footsteps almost unbearable, especially since the last thing I wanted was to be on a farm. "Have you been drinking?" he asks, smelling the whiskey on me. "You aren't even twenty-one." He smirks. "I'm telling Mom."

I shake my head, smirking back at him. "She was there when Grandpa gave it to me." I puff out my chest and fold my arms.

He groans. "Is she still crying?" He looks around the bar to see if he can spot her. "She called me all week to tell me that she misses me." He puts his head back and exhales. "I live five minutes away from her." Grabbing his bottle of beer, he brings it to his mouth. "All kidding aside," he says, "you stay fucking safe out there." He stands taller at six foot four to my six foot two, and where he is blond with blue eyes, I have black hair with blue eyes.

"I'll try my best," I say, and he hugs me. "See you tomorrow morning." I know he'll be at my house for the big breakfast my mother makes.

The rest of the night is spent saying goodbye to all my family. Lots of tears from some and then smiles from the rest. "Tonight was good," I say, sitting at the bar watching Amelia and Asher clean up. Usually, I would be helping, but I gave up the job two weeks ago. "I mean, I got more lovin' than I'm used to." I look over at Amelia and wink.

"Okay, big boy, time for you to go," Amelia says, putting down the rag she's using to clean the bar.

I look around the empty bar, and all these emotions are hitting me. Emotions I'm shocked to feel. "Where the hell is Hazel?" I've known Hazel my whole life. Our grandfathers were even friends when they were in high school. Since she started working here a couple of months ago, we have been getting closer, but she is leaving for college in two months.

"She took the night off," Amelia says, not looking at me. "It was supposed to be just family and friends tonight. She didn't want to impose, so I gave her the night off." The disappointment hits me more than I expected it to.

I tap my finger on the bar. "Okay, I'm out. See you all tomorrow." Getting up, I walk out of the bar.

The hot air hits me right away. I start to take the path I've taken for the past two months that leads straight to Hazel's house. I take my phone out of my pocket and text her.

Me: Where are you?

I wait for her to answer me, but all it says is delivered. I finally get to the clearing and see her house is all dark. Usually, her grandfather leaves a light on for her or waits up for her on the porch. This time, though, everything is off, but I still make my way over to her window. I don't know if it's the fact I'm leaving tomorrow or if it's the whiskey in me, but the urge to see her is strong. I pick up a little pebble and toss it at her window, missing it by a mile but hitting the wood.

I duck down in case her grandfather hears the noise and gets up to chase me with a shotgun. I think about picking up more rocks but then decide just to call her.

Pulling out the phone from my pocket, I call her, and she answers in a groggy voice after the second ring.

"Hello," she grumbles.

"Hey," I say, smiling when I hear her voice. "It's me."

"I have caller ID, Reed," she says, and I hear the rustling of her covers. "What time is it?"

"A little after midnight," I say, looking up at her window. "Why didn't you come to my party?" I ask.

"I don't know. I thought it was for family. What difference does it make?"

"I'm outside," I say, my eyes never leaving her window.

"Outside where?" she asks. I hear her getting up and see a light coming toward the window. I see her silhouette, and I hold up my hand with a smile. "Oh my God," she says, pushing her window up. "What the hell are you doing here?"

"I wanted to see you," I answer, then hang up the phone. "Come sit with me."

"It's the middle of the night," she huffs. "You are crazy, Reed."

"Spend my last night with me." I put my hands in my back pockets, and my heart starts to speed up as I look at her. She turns around and closes the window.

"Does that mean she's coming?" I ask the universe, and a couple of minutes later, I hear the front door open softly. I walk over to the porch and see her quietly close the door behind her, the smile on my face hurting my cheeks when she looks over at me.

"What the hell?" she says, coming down the steps.

She's wearing shorts and a tank top with a flannel button-down tied around her waist. "Why couldn't you just go home?" She steps closer to me. "What is that smell?" She scrunches up her nose, and I know her hazel eyes are browner at night than during the day. "Is that whiskey?"

I grab her hand and pull her with me toward her grandfather's barn. "It's my grandfather's whiskey," I say as we walk side by side, her hand slipping out of mine. When I've walked her home the past couple of weeks, we would go into the barn and talk for most of the night. "We were celebrating." I look over at her as we walk through the grass toward the red barn. "You would know that had you shown up." I push her shoulder with mine.

She doesn't look over at me. Instead, she continues to look down at the ground and shrugs. "Didn't think it would be that big of a deal that I wasn't there." Her voice is soft, and I slide the barn door open just enough for us to slip in. She makes her way over to the side and starts climbing the wooden ladder up to the loft. Nothing but hay and a flannel blanket are up there. "I should have worn pants," she says, going to sit down on the blanket, and all I see are her long legs as she crosses them. "This time tomorrow, you'll be in a single bed."

I sit in front of her, my legs stretched sideways next to her, and lean back on my arms. "I know," I say excitedly. "I can't wait."

"So I've heard." She breaks into a huge smile. "You might have mentioned it a time or two." She lies down and looks up at the window. I lie down beside her, looking up at the stars.

"Aren't you excited to leave?" I ask, and she just nods her head.

"But I'll miss home," she says softly. "I'll miss my pops." She turns to look at me. "There has to be something you are going to miss."

"My family," I answer right away. "Without a doubt, that is the only thing I'll miss from this town." I look back up at the twinkling stars in the sky. "I just don't fit in," I tell her my deepest secret. "Being a farm boy is never the life I wanted, but it's all I know." I look at her and see that she's looking up at the stars. "Yet it's what I hate the most." I turn back to look at the stars. "It's suffocating."

"It's because there are so many of you." She laughs at her own joke.

"I want to see what else is out there." I put one hand on my stomach. "I want to travel and see the world. If I stay here." I look at her, and she turns her soft hazel eyes toward me. "I'll die a little each day." She is the most beautiful girl I know, and she doesn't even know it. "Thank you," I say, turning on my side now. "For being there these last couple of months." My hand comes up to touch her face. "I just have one regret."

"Really?" she says. "You said you never have regrets." She throws my words in my face.

"Well, I have now." I smirk. "Don't you want to know what it is?"

"I'm dying with anticipation," she says, and I don't think I've ever not laughed when I've been around her.

"That we didn't get close sooner," I say, licking my lips. My stomach dips as I look at her eyes go just a touch lighter. She looks down now, almost afraid of me seeing her. "Look at me," I say. She looks up at me, and I can see the tears in her eyes. "Are those tears for me? You continue like that …" I try to joke, ignoring the pull at my chest. "Then I'm going to think you like me." She moves her hand to push me, but I grab it and pull her closer to me. "I'm going to miss you, Hazel." I've practiced saying that since last week but have been too chicken to say it out loud. "I'm going to miss you the most, I think." My voice trails off into a whisper.

"I'm going to miss you, too, Reed," she says softly. "Very much so." I release her hand, and it drops onto the hay. I lean my head in, and she meets me halfway, her lips meeting mine. Her tongue slides in to tangle with mine, and I roll her on her back. I can't believe I've waited this long to kiss her. I can't believe I've finally gotten the courage, and I'm leaving tomorrow. I've waited for this moment for what feels like my whole life. She melts in my arms, and I swear I'll remember this for years to come.

There in the middle of the barn, I have her for the first time. We spent the night getting lost in each other until the sunshine starts to pour into the barn. I stand and put my shirt on, holding out my hand for her. She slips her hand in mine, and we slowly make our way out of the barn.

I hold her neck in my hands as I give her one last kiss. "You should get going before my grandfather comes out," she says, and I nod, turning to walk away from her.

I turn back to face her, walking backward. "You, Hazel Bennett"—I smirk—"are the best thing this town has given me." I hold my hands out to my sides.

I watch her smile one last time before I walk away from her and this town.

One

REED

Six years later

AFTER PARKING THE Jeep in the same spot I always park in, I turn it off and open the door. A hiss leaves my mouth when I stretch my leg and pull the stitches tight. "Motherfucker," I say, getting out of the truck and slamming the door.

I walk slower than I want to, but the fact that I'm walking without a cane right now is a big deal. Even though they pushed it on me, I refused it every time. I was just going to push myself harder.

Eight weeks and three days ago, we were ambushed in our convoy. I close my eyes, and all I can hear is the sound of whizzing as the bomb came straight for us. I was pinned under the truck. I felt the metal pieces all the way down to my bone and knew I should have stayed put. I also knew that if I did stay put, I would die, so I ripped my leg from under the truck. I felt the bullets whizz by all of us, and I could call for close air support to assist in pushing back the assault. I would do what I needed to do to make sure we all left here together.

Heading up the concrete walkway, I pull open the glass door. I nod to a couple of the guys while I make my way down the white corridor. My heart beats erratically in my chest. I feel like I did when I first joined six years ago. I had no idea what or how long I would be in the military, but I fell in love with it and knew this is where I was meant to be. In ninety days, I'll sign on for another four years.

I get to my commander's door and raise my hand to knock. "Enter." When I hear him speak, I open the door. He looks up, and a smile spreads across his face. "Staff Sergeant Barnes." He gets up from his chair and comes over to me, holding out his hand for me to shake.

"Lieutenant Colonel Rizzotto." I say his name, shaking his hand since he extended his hand to me first.

"You're looking good." He looks down at my leg. "I heard it was tough."

"I'm fine," I say, and he gestures to the empty chair in front of his desk. I sit down, and my good leg starts to bounce as I wait for him to round his desk and have a seat. "Like I told the doctors in Germany, I'm good to go." I look at him.

"From what I read, you and your squad were all

accounted for with zero casualties." He leans back in his chair. "And from the pictures I've seen, it's a miracle." I nod at him, not adding anything else to it.

"I'm ready to get back to duty," I say. My leg clenches at the same time as I say it, but I push it back.

"I read that, too." He puts his hands on his desk and entwines his fingers. "But I also got the report from the doctors."

I sit up. "All I need is some extra physical therapy, and I'll be all good."

"And that is what you are going to get," he says. "I'm not going to beat around the bush. You know better than anyone that I also have my orders. And as per the doctors, you aren't as ready as you want to be."

"I might be a bit slow," I say. Deep down, I know I'm not ready, but admitting it will be harder to do.

"You are going on convalescent leave." He says the two words I've been dreading. "Come back in thirty days, and we'll assess you again. I have no doubt you'll be good to go, and you can sign that next contract with us." He smiles, and I nod. One thing I know is that you never go against the doctor's orders.

"Yes sir," I say even though my heart is breaking. For the past six years, this is all I've known. This is all I've wanted.

"I'm looking forward to having you back." We stand, and I shake his hand.

"I'll be back better than ever," I tell him, walking out of the room and shutting the door behind me softly.

The phone rings in my back pocket. Taking it out, I

see it's my father. "Hello," I say, answering him as I walk out of the building.

"Hey," he says. "I was wondering if you were going to send me to voice mail," he jokes.

"I did that one time, Dad," I say. "One time three years ago."

"And I'm still holding it over your head." He laughs now. "How did the meeting go?"

"I'm on convalescent leave," I say, and the words are bitter in my mouth. It's going to be a tough pill to swallow.

"What are you going to do?" he asks as I open my truck door.

"What do you mean?"

"Why don't you come home?" His voice goes soft. "I'll set everything up here for a physical therapist to work with you. You can even stay in the white house. You know that no one will bother you there." I laugh, knowing he is right. No one likes going there because it's like a museum. He's bargaining with me because I haven't been home since I left all those years ago. Not once. "You know Grandma and Grandpa have been asking for you."

Starting my truck, I look out at the green trees and hear honking in the distance. "You have thirty days," he says, and I close my eyes.

"Fine," I say, and I can hear him cheer from here. "Let me get my shit together, and then I'll message you when I land."

"You call me when your shit is ready," my father says.

"I'll get you a plane."

"Fine," I say, knowing I won't be able to argue with him, and if I do, he'll get on the plane and come and get me himself. I hang up the phone and make my way over to the house I share with five other fellow soldiers.

We are never here all at the same time, so it works out for us. I walk up the steps one at a time because my leg burns. Opening my door, I grab my green duffel bag and put my clothes in it. My phone rings again, and looking down, I see it's my brother.

"Dad call you?" I ask, laughing. It's good to hear his voice.

"No," he says. "I was with him when he called you. Gotta say I thought he was going to cry."

"I've been telling you this my whole life." I grab my T-shirts. "I'm his favorite."

"Harlow is his favorite," he says. "Only because she won't move out of the house."

"What the fuck is she still doing living at home?" I ask, shocked.

"Why don't you ask her when you get here?" he says. "You need anything?"

"Nah, I think I'll be good," I say. "Are you with Dad?"

"He's in the barn, why?" he asks.

"Tell him I'll be ready in ten minutes," I say, and he laughs.

"The plane was ready five seconds after you hung up on him. I'll send you the information."

"Figures," I say, turning now to sit on my bed. "See you soon."

"Fly safe," he says and disconnects. The ping of a text comes through right after with the address of the private airfield.

I exhale, looking around the bare room. I haven't really done much to it, the only personal things I have are the pictures on my dresser of some of the places I've visited.

Getting up, I take one more look around. "Be back in twenty-nine days," I tell the bare walls. As I'm leaving, I run into one of my roommates.

"Hey, where are you off to?" he asks, looking at my bag slung over my shoulder.

"Home," I say, and his eyes go big. "It's been a while."

"When are you coming back?" he asks.

"Not sure yet. But by next month," I say. "See you then." I look down when I get a text from my father.

Dad: Car is out waiting for you. No rush.

"My car is here," I say. "Take care."

"Stay safe." I salute him as I walk out of the house. The car is parked out front, and the driver gets out to grab my bag.

"I got it," I say, and he waits for me to put the bag in the trunk. He holds the door open for me, and I get in. We don't chitchat as he drives to the airfield where the private plane is waiting for me. My heartbeat speeds up as I get closer, and I want to tell the driver to take me back. Maybe going to visit right now isn't a good idea.

I get out and meet the driver at the trunk, but someone is already there to grab my bag. "Welcome, Mr. Barnes," he says, and not hearing my rank of staff sergeant in front is weird.

I walk up the five little stairs and duck down to get into the plane, and the flight attendant is there smiling at me. “Welcome aboard,” she says. “We’ll get off the ground as soon as you’re seated.”

I walk to the chair with a nod, then sit down and look out the little window. The plane prepares for takeoff, and I see the car drive away. I look out the window as we take off, and when she comes back with a tray of fruit, I just smile at her and ask for water.

My whole body is tight with nerves. I roll my neck, but my stomach gets tighter. As we get closer and closer to landing, my whole body trembles. My leg bounces, and when the wheels touch down, I feel like I’m going to vomit. “It’s just for a month,” I remind myself, mentally preparing for the guilt and the questions on why I haven’t come back. Because the only answer I have will make me feel like an asshole.

I wait for the door to open before I get up. After thanking her, I walk out of the plane, and the humidity hits me right away. I walk down the five steps and see a black Range Rover waiting off to the side.

When the driver’s side opens, and I see dirty cowboy boots, I smile. Only my father can pull this shit off. His jeans are even worse than his boots. His whole fucking face lights up when he sees me. He walks over to me with tears in his eyes. Grabbing my shoulder in his hand, he pulls me to him, giving me the biggest hug he’s ever given me in my life. He puts his hand on the back of my head, letting me go from the hug. Gazing into his blue eyes is like looking in a mirror. “Welcome home, son.”

Two

Hazel

THE SOFT ALARM wakes me, and I stick out my arm to grab my phone. I bring the phone with me under the covers and debate if I should get up and work out or just get the extra hour of sleep. I close my eyes, and when the second alarm wakes me, I throw the covers off me and get up.

It's still dark outside, but the sun is slowly starting to rise. I walk over to the chair in my room, slipping out of my shorts and tank top and replacing it with my yoga pants and sports bra. I grab my water bottle out of the fridge and walk to the exercise bike in the corner of the living room. Turning the television on low, I start riding the bike, and forty-five minutes later, I'm heaving while I walk down the hallway.

Stopping in front of the closed door and opening it, I see it's still a bit dark in the room. My daughter, Sofia, sleeps in the middle of the bed with the covers kicked off. I pull the door just a bit even though she should be getting up any second now. She has her own alarm clock, and every day at six thirty, she is out of bed. Even when she was born five years ago, six thirty was her time. No matter what time she goes to bed, it's her inner clock.

I step into the shower, and like clockwork, I hear her walking in right when I'm drying myself off. "Momma." She rubs her eyes as she comes to me.

I look up at my twin and smile. "Morning, baby," I say, softly kissing her neck. "How did you sleep?"

"Good," she grumbles. "I had a dream of clowns and horses."

I laugh. "Did the clowns ride the horses?" I ask, and she giggles. "Why don't you go get dressed, and I'll start breakfast."

"Okay, Momma." She stops in front of me again so I can kiss her. "I want pancakes."

"Okay," I say, kissing her on the lips now and watching her bounce off to get dressed.

I slip on my robe and walk to the kitchen of my condo, opening the shades to allow the sunlight to pour in.

I never thought I'd be a single mom. Not me. I had a plan, and none of that was me being a teenage mom. I could have given up then and there, but instead, it pushed me harder. Not only did I want to achieve big things but I also wanted to do it for Sofia. I never ever wanted her to miss anything, never wanted her to have that thought in her head that because I had her, my dreams were crushed.

So I put my head down and took extra business classes to make sure I would be okay when I gave birth. I took three weeks off and then jumped back into school. My grandfather covered all the daycare bills for Sofia, and I had a small trust fund from when my parents passed away to help with expenses.

My grandfather was my saving grace. I was so scared to tell him I was pregnant and see the disappointment in his eyes. When I was four years old, I was in the car with my parents when they were struck by a drunk driver. They hit a tree head-on, and the only ones who walked away from the accident with no scratches were the drunk driver and me. That day, he lost his only daughter, who he raised by himself after my grandmother passed away from an aneurysm when my mother was ten, and gained me.

"I'm dressed," Sofia says, walking into the room wearing her private school outfit of a pleated skirt and a white polo shirt. She walks over to one of the stools and hops up on it as I take the strawberries out of the fridge and put some on a plate for her.

"Ohh, my favorite," she says, clapping her hands. "Thank you, Momma."

I rush to make her the pancakes she wants while I mix myself a protein smoothie. I leave her to eat while I walk back to my bedroom and get dressed. I slip on a pair of black pants with a short-sleeved black shirt with white vertical and horizontal lines. Slipping on my black shoes, I walk to the bathroom to apply some mascara and then untie my hair from the ponytail, brushing it once. I'm walking out when my phone rings with a fifteen-minute warning. "Let's go," I say, returning to the kitchen to see Sofia putting her empty plate in the sink. "Go brush your teeth," I say. "I'll get your lunch." I put my smoothie cup in the sink and rinse it out, then turn to grab both of our lunch boxes out of the fridge.

She skips off to brush her teeth while I put everything in the dishwasher and start it. I walk to the bathroom and find her finishing. I grab the hairbrush. "Two ponytails or one?" I ask, and she holds up two fingers. I brush her brown hair and put it up in pigtails. "Shoes," I say when the phone alerts me with a five-minute timer.

I find her at the front door, slipping on her blue Mary Jane shoes, strapping the Velcro herself. I grab her schoolbag with my purse and the two lunch boxes on my way out of the house. She stops right beside me while I lock the door and holds my free hand as we walk over to my truck. I press the unlock button to open the back door, and she climbs into her booster seat. I watch her buckle herself in while I put our bags in the front passenger seat. I close the door and make my way to the driver's side.

Pulling out of the complex, I make my way over to her school. "Momma," she calls out, and I look at her through the rearview mirror. "Can we go to the beach this weekend?" she asks, looking out her window.

"We can see," I say. "We have to go visit a couple of camps. Summer is right around the corner."

"Can we go to the beach after?" she asks, and I smile over at her. When the sun hits her eyes, I can see her father in her.

"Probably," I say, pulling up to her school and parking. I get out, then walk over and grab her bag out of the front seat before opening the back door for her. She jumps out, and I hand her the backpack and lunch box. I hold her hand as we walk toward the playground. Kids are running and playing, and a couple of the little girls call her name.

Stopping outside of the gate, I squat down in front of her, and my heart fills with so much love. "Have the best day." Tapping her nose with my finger, I hug her and kiss her once, then she turns to walk into the schoolyard. I get up and watch her play with her friends, making a couple of to-do lists in my head.

"Morning." I hear a mom beside me and look over to see the head of the PTA approaching. "I was hoping I would see you this morning," she says, smiling, and all of her screams fake. "We are having a bake sale at the end of the month, and we were wondering if you could possibly make your special cupcakes and cookies."

"Sure," I say. "I'll do a dozen of each."

She claps her hands. "That's fantastic," she says. The bell rings, and I watch Sofia line up. Only when she walks inside do I turn and walk back to the truck.

It takes me ten minutes to get to work, which is another reason I chose the school. Parking in the underground parking, I get out and walk over to the elevator. I press the button for the tenth floor when I step in all by myself.

When the elevator doors open again, the wall-to-wall windows on this floor fill the area with light. "Morning,

Sara," I say to the receptionist when I walk in and head down the gray carpet to my little office. I put my purse on my desk, then go to the communal kitchen and put my bag in the fridge. Grabbing a mug, I fill it with coffee and walk back to my office.

I sit down and turn on my computer, seeing the company logo boot up right away. I graduated with a bachelor's degree in business in three years instead of the usual four, then took additional courses to graduate and pass the CPA. It was lots of sleepless nights and lots of sacrifices and tears on both sides. Thinking back now, I don't know how I did it. I think it was the sheer determination mixed with the fact I couldn't let my grandfather down again.

Luckily, the company where I was doing my internship was expanding their office, so they reached out and offered me a job I couldn't refuse. I could start after dropping Sofia off at school, and I could leave at four.

A picture of me graduating with Sofia in my arms and my grandfather beside me sits on my desk. I check my emails, making sure my clients have sent me all the papers I need in order to close the files for the month. I don't even realize how much time has passed when the phone rings. "Hello." I put the phone to my ear, looking at my screen.

"Is this Hazel Bennett?" the male voice asks, and I don't know why everything in me stops moving.

"This is she," I say, listening to a voice I've never heard before. A voice that will change my life.

"This is Dr. Shepard." He says his name, and everything around me feels like it's spinning.

"I'm sorry." I find the words lodged in my throat. "I don't know a Dr. Shepard."

I hear him breathe out. "I'm a friend and doctor to your grandfather, Kaine Johnson," he says, and my stomach sinks.

"Is my grandfather okay?" I ask, the panic apparent in my voice.

"I'm so sorry to do this to you over the phone," he says, and the tears start. "Your grandfather has passed away."

"What?" I ask in a whisper. "When?" I wipe the tear off my cheek. "I spoke to him two days ago, and he was fine."

"He had stage four small cell carcinoma," he says in a soothing voice.

"I had no idea." My heart breaks in my chest, knowing that, besides Sofia, my last family member I have is gone. "He never said anything."

"He's been sick a while, but he's been struggling for the past six months," he says, filling me in, all I can do is sit there numb.

"He was admitted into the hospital last week for complications, and we found out it had spread."

I close my eyes, and all I can see is my grandfather and his big smile. I put my hand in front of my mouth. "Was anyone with him when he passed away?" I ask, and it takes him a couple of minutes to answer me.

"He passed in his sleep," he says, and I try to hide my

sob. "He had a DNR, and he also refused to let anyone see him like that. The funeral home has picked him up, and he's being cremated this evening." I don't say anything because I can't. I can't say anything. "I'm so sorry for your loss, Hazel," Dr. Shepard says. "He loved you and Sofia with everything he had."

"Thank you," I say, "for letting me know."

"If you have any questions or if you need anything …" He gives me his number, which I don't take down. Hanging up the phone, I'm staring at my desk when someone walks by my office and notices me crying.

"Are you okay?" Caitlyn says, and I just look at her because the shock is still settling in.

"My grandfather passed away," I say, and she puts her hand to her mouth.

"Oh my gosh, is there anything I can do?" she asks.

I look at her, saying the words I said I would never say. "I have to go home."

Three

Reed

"KEEP YOUR HEAD up." I looked around at my squad as they all nodded at me. We walked down the street, and rubble was everywhere. "Eyes open," I told them as the five of us walked side by side. We took in the shattered storefronts.

"They did this to their own people," one of my guys said in disbelief, and I just looked over at him, I held the gun in my hand as we walked past what looks like a church. A couple of people are now in the street with us.

Out of the corner of my eye, I spotted a little girl with brown hair, she looked straight at me. My breath stopped as she turned and walked into the building. My feet moved as I followed her and called out. "Stop," I said, knowing she wasn't going to understand. She walked into the front door, and when I got in there, I saw baby bassinets everywhere. I stopped in the middle of the room, my body bent over to pick up a disregarded doll. The blond hair was matted, and she had burn marks all over her, the plastic melted in some spots. Movement to the side made me look back at the little girl who stood there and smiled at me. I looked into her eyes and then saw the grenade in her hand as she dropped it on the floor. I yelled right before it exploded.

I gasp as if I just came up from holding my breath underwater. Sitting up in the bed, I feel wetness all around me. It takes a second for me to gather my bearings and remember where I am. Using the light from the bathroom, I see that I'm in a king-size bed. "Home," I say to myself. "I'm home." I look down, and drops of sweat drip off me.

Swinging my legs off the bed, I look down at the pink and snarly scar on my leg that goes from the middle of my thigh to my knee. I get up, and the skin pulls tight as I walk over to the bathroom and dim the lights. After turning the shower on, I turn to look at myself in the mirror. My eyes go to the scar on my side that I got while on a training exercise, making me think back.

I arrived at base more excited than I've ever been in all my life. Arriving in Georgia, I couldn't wait to start and woke up before everyone else. It was a sixty-two-day Ranger program, and I finished at the top of my class. My body had bulked up during this. I closed myself off from my family and my life back at home, deleting all forms of social media and even suspending my cell phone. I called home once a week on Sunday using the base phone, but other than that, my life was on training. I worked my way up the ranks and trained with some of the baddest sons of bitches who ever walked the earth. I would die for each of my brothers, and I knew they would for me, too.

When I went on my first deployment, I got another cell phone, but I drew the line at social media until Quinn and Willow had a baby. I followed just my family, and by then, my life was very different from theirs. They followed me as I toured the world, and to be honest, in the past six years, I've missed them a total of two times—on my first Christmas without them and when Harlow graduated. Other than that, I was okay.

I hang my head as the water streams over me, my eyes closing when I see that little girl again, and I quickly open my eyes.

"The mind is a tricky place," the psychiatrist said when I went in for a mandatory evaluation after I arrived in Germany. "Sometimes, it locks memories, only for them to come out when we least expect it."

Turning the shower off, I grab a white towel and wrap it around my waist, walking from the master bedroom toward the kitchen. Turning on the lights and looking at the kitchen, I shake my head. My mother has definitely renovated this kitchen in the past two years. Everything is white.

The massive island in the middle of the room has a marble white and gray countertop with three silver lights hanging over it. I walk to one of the cupboards and open it, trying to find coffee. Once I do, I start the coffee and walk back to the bedroom, slipping on a pair of boxers and shorts. The aroma of coffee fills the house, and I grab a mug to fill up.

Walking out to the backyard, I sit on the porch step and look up at the sky. The black sky is turning a soft gray right before it turns a soft pink. I try not to think about the last time I saw this sky. I try not to think about Hazel and the last time I saw these stars. I put her back in the safe box of memories I'll take to the grave. I drink my coffee, watching the sun wake up and shine down.

Getting up, I walk back inside, my stomach now rumbling a little. Opening the big stainless steel fridge, I see that it's full. I also see that my grandmother has sent over some of my favorite food. I start taking out the chicken potpie when I hear the sound of a car door shut. I look over at the clock on the stove and see that it's a little after seven.

"Welcome home." I shake my head when I hear the soft knock on the door. Walking to the door, I open it, and a smile fills my face when I see my cousin Ethan there. "This fucking guy," he says, looking at me. "Holy shit, you grew." He holds up his hand. "I've got breakfast."

I move to the side. "Come in," I say, and when he comes through the doorway, he stops and gives me a hug.

"Glad to have you home," he says, and I nod.

"It's good to be home." The words taste sour in my mouth. "I think," I say, shaking my head. Out of everyone here, Ethan is the one who might understand me the most. He left home when he was twenty-one, and no one saw him for seven years.

I close the door and walk into the kitchen with him. "You were going to eat chicken potpie at seven in the morning?"

"I haven't had that in six years," I say, laughing. "Fucking right, I was going to eat it at seven a.m."

"Then I guess you don't want what's in the bag?" He holds up the big brown bag in his hands.

"What's in the bag?" I ask, and he laughs.

"Grandma's biscuits and gravy that she just made," he says, and my mouth waters just thinking about it.

"I'll have that on the side with the chicken potpie," I say, walking over to get plates out. I scoop some pie and pop it in the microwave. "Do you want some coffee?"

"Sure, I'll have a cup," he says. I can tell he wants me to be comfortable with him. I pour him a cup of coffee and another one for myself.

He walks over to the fridge and takes the milk out to pour in his coffee. Pulling out the stool at the counter, he sits down, opens the bag, and takes out two containers.

I grab two forks and hand him one as I sit next to him. Opening my container, I moan when I see the food. "You can't get this anywhere," Ethan says, taking a bite. "No matter where you travel to."

I cut my own piece and close my eyes when the buttery biscuit hits my tongue. The richness of the gravy hits my tongue next along with the little pieces of sausage. "This is the best thing I've ever had." I chew and then take a bite of the potpie. "And this."

"Nothing," he says, taking his own bite. "And I mean

nothing is like home cooking." He takes a couple more bites, and neither of us says anything. "So what did they do?"

"Convalescent leave," I answer, not looking at him. "Doctor's orders."

"Gives you extra time to heal," he says. "Nothing wrong with that."

"I have a training session at nine and then at three," I say. "I'll be fine."

"What about talking to someone?" he asks, and I look over at him. "I needed all the help I could get when I got home. No one knew but me," he tells me. "I would sit with this guy who didn't even say a word back to me. He just let me talk." He finishes chewing and then swallows. "Might do you good."

"Maybe," I say, avoiding his eyes. "I get re-evaluated in thirty days."

"When is your contract up?" My sip of coffee suddenly tastes bitter on the way down.

"Ninety days," I say.

"Then what are you going to do?" he asks, and I look at him.

"With what?" My leg begins to shake. This is why I didn't want to come back home. I knew I'd feel guilty when I left them again.

"Are you going to give them another four years?" he asks, and I nod.

"Fucking right," I say, getting up. "Wouldn't want to do anything else."

"Have you tried to do anything else?" he asks, and I

shrug.

"The farm life might be good for some people," I say to him. "But not me. I hate it here. I always did."

"You hated it when you were eighteen," he says. "Who knows how you feel now. Things change. People change."

"I know one thing," I say. "In ninety days, I'm signing another contract." He just stares at me. "I know that this"—I stretch my hands—"is not where I want to end up."

"Well, you're here for the month," he tells me. "Why don't you put that chip away and enjoy your family?"

"I don't have a chip," I say, and he laughs.

"You have a chip so big on that shoulder, it's holding you down." He pushes away from the counter. "Trust me, I know. I had the same one."

"I'm not you," I say, and he just smirks.

"We are all the same," he says. "I have to go get my kids to school." He nods at me. "See you at nine."

"What?" I ask, surprised.

"Who the fuck you think is going to train your pussy ass." He laughs now. "And don't think I'm going to go easy on you either."

I clap my hands together. "You sure you got it in you, old man?" I bait him, and he flips me the bird.

"I'll remember that when I push you so hard you cry," he says, turning and walking toward the door.

He stops and turns. "Welcome home, Reed." I don't say anything else to him. He walks out of the house, slamming the door behind him.

“Twenty-eight more days,” I say out loud. “And this place will be a memory once again.” I’m nervous about being home and having to answer the questions that might come my way. The biggest one being what took me so long to return.

Four

Hazel

THE CLOCK ON the radio tells me that it is just past one in the morning. Looking in the rearview mirror, I see that Sofia has fallen asleep. The lone tear runs down my face when I realize I'll be back home in an hour.

After I hung up the phone with the doctor, I went to see my boss. I knocked on his door, and he looked up. He was the one I worked closely with during my internship and offered me the job. His smile quickly faded when he saw my face.

"Come sit." He ushered me in.

"Thank you," I told him, but I stood instead. I was afraid that if I sat down, I would curl up into a ball and sob.

"I just got a call that my grandfather passed." The

words coming out of my mouth were still surreal.

"Oh, no." He walked around his desk to hug me. "I'm so, so sorry. What can we do to help?" he asked.

"I'll have to go home to handle his affairs," I told him, and he just nodded.

"Whatever time you need, you take it," he said. "We are already up to speed with all your work."

I swallowed down the lump in my throat. "Thank you. I will know more when I'm there." I left his office, and it didn't take me long to close up my files.

I arrived at Sofia's school early and took her out of class. Her teacher was very sympathetic and told me she would email me stuff to help keep her busy. I kept my sunglasses on the whole time as I spoke with her.

Once we got home, I took them off, and that was when Sofia noticed.

"Why you crying, Momma?" she said, coming over to me and hugging my hips. "You want to eat ice cream?" she asked, and I smiled down at her.

I brought her to the couch and sat with her on my lap and told her that Pops had gone to heaven. She didn't really understand, and I knew this because as I packed our bags, she asked me if Pops would take her on the tractor. When he would visit they would spend hours talking about the tractor from home. It was her favorite thing in the world to talk with him about. There is a picture by her bed with him on his red tractor, and every single time he came to visit us, she would ask about that tractor.

I shut off my mind as I packed the car, then made

sure she had her iPad fully charged, and we were off. It was an eight-hour drive without stopping. We only lasted forty minutes until she had to pee, and then after another hour, she was hungry. Needless to say, it was going to take us ten hours with all the stops we made.

The GPS tells me that my exit is coming up, and when I look up, my chest starts to get even tighter. I've spent this whole drive with tears running down my face, replaying the memories of Pops and me. Growing up, I never lacked anything, and he made sure he was there for me every single step of the way.

I think back to the last words he said to me. "I love you till the end of time." If only I knew it was the last time, I would have spent more time talking to him to ask him all the questions.

I roll my lips to stop the sob when I get off the exit. The familiar trees make me close my eyes and take a deep breath. The same trees from when I left six years ago and vowed never to come back.

No one is on the road in town, and I look around at how much it's changed. The diner is still there, but a couple of cute little stores are next to it. One looks like an ice cream shop, and the other looks like a hairdresser right next to what looks like a spa.

I drive past the sheriff's department and then the bar, but it's closed. My heart pounds in my chest, and my breathing comes in slow spurts. "Relax," I tell myself. "It's only two weeks. I'll be gone before anyone asks any questions."

Turning down the dark road that leads to the house,

I can't help the sob that rips through me. I put my hand to my mouth as the house comes into view. This time, there's no light on to welcome me home like he always used to do.

I park in front of the house and see that the grass is longer than he would ever keep it. The landscaping in the front is overgrown with weeds. I look in the back seat at Sofia, who is still sleeping. Getting out of the truck, I grab my keys and walk up the two steps that lead to the porch. His rocking chair rocks with the soft breeze. "Hey, Pops," I say to myself.

After unlocking the door, I return to the truck to grab Sofia. I unbuckle her, and she wakes up. "Are we here?" She rubs her eyes.

"We are, baby." I kiss her cheek and take her in my arms. She places her head on my shoulder. Putting a hand on her back, I walk back up the steps, and my eyes turn to look at the chair, somehow hoping he would be there.

Walking into the house, I'm expecting it to be exactly like it was the last time. But it's not. Nothing is like it was. The living room is gone, and in its place is a hospital bed. If I wasn't holding Sofia, I would have fallen to my knees.

A lone chair sits by his bed, and I wonder if he had someone who looked after him. I wonder if he had someone come by and talk to him. I shake my head, angry he didn't let me help him and went through all that alone without his family. Walking toward the stairs, I see that a layer of dust coats the picture frames. The stairs creak while I walk up to go to my old room.

My queen bed sits in the middle of the room with a white sheet over it. It's exactly like I left it six years ago. The clothes that I left on the chair in the corner are still folded. I walk over to the corner of the sheet and slowly remove it, dropping it to the floor.

Picking up a pillow, I smell it before putting Sofia down on the bed. I pull the covers to the side and place her down. She turns on her side and falls back asleep right away. I tuck her in, kissing her cheek softly.

Walking down the stairs, I go to grab our stuff out of my truck, and when I stop to look up at the house, I see it's almost in shambles. My grandfather would never ever have let it get this bad.

Carrying the bag up to my room, I place it down in the corner. I look out the window, letting my eyes adjust to the darkness. Walking back downstairs to finish unloading the car, I close the front door and refuse to look over at the hospital bed.

I kick off my shoes and collapse on the bed beside Sofia. When I push her hair away from her face, she turns, and I pull her into my arms, and my eyes close.

My heavy eyes flicker open and then close again, my body aching when I feel a head on my stomach because Sofia is sleeping like an octopus. I try to go back to sleep, but I need to pee. I slip out of bed and go to the bathroom, then wash my face. I grab a towel, and the minute I bring it to my face, I smell my grandfather. I bring it closer to my face as the tears come.

When I walk out of the bathroom and down the stairs, the sunlight is starting to come in through the windows, and I stop in my tracks. It's dirty and dusty, and I know that I will spend the greater part of today cleaning this mess.

The kitchen is not as bad as the rest of the house. I open the fridge and see it's almost empty. The freezer is filled with microwave meals he used to hate, and I shake my head. Turning, I make myself a coffee.

I grab my mug and open the back door, stepping outside. The deck looks like the wood is rotting. I walk to the step and sit down, the whole time holding my breath, hoping I don't fucking fall through it.

Birds fly over me, and their chirping makes me look toward the barn. I gasp out in shock when I see its condition. The roof looks like it's fallen in on the right side, and the skylight on the left side looks busted. Bringing the mug to my mouth, I remember the last time I was in that barn.

It was two months after Reed left, and I was leaving the next day to go to college. My stomach had been giving me issues for a month, but I chalked it up to the nerves about leaving home. Only when my phone alerted me that I should be getting my period did I stop and think of the last time I got it. I borrowed Pops' car and drove two towns over to get the pregnancy test, and the bag felt like it weighed a thousand pounds when I walked into the house.

"Did you get everything you needed?" Pops asked me as soon as I kicked off my shoes. My hands trembled, wondering if he was going to ask me what was in the bag.

"Yeah," I said. "I'm going to go make sure I have everything packed." I smiled at him, and I tried to ignore the tears in his eyes.

Going to the bathroom, I read the instructions five times before finally taking the test. Putting it back in the bag, I hid it in my pants when I walked back out of the bathroom.

Pops was in his bedroom, so I made my way out to the barn and opened the door just enough to slip inside. Ever since Reed left, I never came in here anymore because the heartache followed the anger I felt. The memory of that night was still the only thing I dreamed of.

I walked up the ladder and sat down, pulling the brown bag out of my shirt. Taking the test out, I held it in my hand. My eyes fixated on the lines. "One line," I said to myself. "Please just stay one line." I didn't know who I was praying to that night, but whoever it was didn't hear my pleas. The second line came out brighter than the first line. My heart stopped in my chest, and the test dropped out of my hand. I lay down on my back, looking out the window with my hand on my stomach, and I already knew what I was going to do. There was no other choice for me.

"Momma." I hear Sofia's voice. "Are you here?"

Looking over at the barn, I get up and walk back to the door. "Let's get this shit over with."

Five

Reed

"COME ON." ETHAN smirks. "You got more in you than that," he says as he stands over me and pushes me to do another set of eight. My arm muscles scream at me as I push up the last one. I lock the weights in place as my arms fall to the sides, and my eyes close.

"That's enough." I hear Ethan snickering, and I sit up, grabbing my water bottle and drinking from it as my chest heaves.

"What, are you tired?" I tease, and he looks over his shoulder at me. He was not lying when he said he would make me vomit. He pushed me so hard that when I went home, I took a shower sitting down. I got myself something to eat and then collapsed into bed. The dreams never came, and I wonder if it was because I was that exhausted. Whatever it was, it was the first time in over a month I didn't have a nightmare.

"I still got a couple of hours left in me," I say, and my whole body clenches in fear.

"Good," he says. "You can run all that energy off." He points at the treadmills. When Ethan came back home all those years ago, my dad made sure he felt at home. He transformed an old fallen-down barn into a state-of-the-art training facility. The walls are covered in mirrors so you can see what you're doing. The middle of the barn has ten weight machines in the shape of a square that work your core. Five bikes on one side of the wall sit right next to five Stairmasters. Two leg press machines are against the other wall with three punching bags and five treadmills. An empty space all the way at the end has two ropes lying on the floor. I get on the treadmill and run for over forty-five minutes before turning it off and deciding I'm done for the day.

"I'm going to shower and go see Grandpa," I say, and he looks over at me.

Out of everyone, he's the one who has been in my face about things. "Doing visits." He stands with his feet apart and his arms crossed over his chest.

"I saw Quinn yesterday," I say, and he rolls his eyes at me.

"He came to see if it was really you." He points at me and then stares me down. "Why do you hate being here so much?" He doesn't mess with words or sugarcoat anything.

"I don't hate it here," I say and then look at him.

"My whole life, I was Casey's son. The big cowboy tech specialist. In high school, I failed computers. Do you know how that felt? It's like they thought I was my father," I say. "Then it was Quinn's little brother. Can you ride horses like Quinn? Can you walk with the stupid swagger that he walks with?" I make up that last part, and Ethan laughs. "I was never just fucking Reed. Pain in the ass, funny, good-looking Reed." I wink at him, trying to make a joke of it.

"Who the fuck told you that you were good-looking?" He shakes his head, and it's my turn to flip him the bird.

"Day one of training." I lift my hand. "Not one person compared me to anyone. I was just Barnes."

"So did you find out who you were?" he asks, and I look down. "You know who you are," he tells me, walking over and grabbing his truck keys. "It's time to show everyone else." He heads toward the door, sliding on his sunglasses. "And put on a fucking shirt. You aren't a stripper."

I clap my hands. "Don't be envious that I'm better built than you are." He walks out, not saying a word, so I grab my shirt and head back to the house, which is ten steps from the barn.

I shower quickly and slip on jeans and a T-shirt. Grabbing my phone, I see I have a call from my mother and then another couple of texts from some of the guys in my squad. I'll get to those later. Tucking my phone in my back pocket, I make my way over to my grandparents' house. I put my glasses on and wonder if I should take the golf cart to their house or just walk it. Everyone in my family is five minutes away from each other. I opt to take the golf cart when my leg twinges because the path to my grandparents' place is smooth.

When I finally see their house, my chest aches because I spent more time here than in my own. This house brought me so many memories. Every Sunday, my grandparents host a barbecue for the town. When I was growing up, it was my favorite day of the week. The day of the week I found out my brother was better than me at everything. The day of the week I would pretend I didn't care, yet inside, a piece of me died every single fucking time.

I spot my grandfather right away as he walks out of his barn, talking to the guy next to him. My grandfather is in jeans, a button-down shirt, worn cowboy boots, and his cowboy hat on his head.

It takes him a couple of minutes to look over at me, but when he does, his face fills with a giant smile, and I can't help but mirror his look. Stopping the golf cart, I get out and walk over to him. "Finally," he says. Coming to me, he grabs my neck and pulls me to him. I hug him just like I did six years ago when I left. "Took you long enough." After slapping my back, he lets me go. His eyes are on mine. "It's been two days."

"I know," I say. The guilt washes over me when he lets me go, and I look over at the man next to him.

"Christopher?" I ask, confused, and he just smirks at me. He's wearing dress pants, a button-up shirt, and a sport coat.

"Son of a bitch," he says, laughing. "Never thought

I'd see this ugly face again." He looks back at my grandfather. "Sorry for swearing." We are twenty-five years old and still afraid to swear in front of my grandfather.

"Me?" I say, pointing at myself. "What the fuck are you wearing?"

"I had patients today," he says, and I look at him confused.

"Patients?" I question him. When I left town, he was headed to community college to go into agriculture.

"It's Doctor now," he says to me, and I just look at him shocked. "I was here to see if my girl could start riding."

"Your girl?" It's only then that I realize how much has changed and how much of a stranger everyone is to me. In shutting myself off from them, I realize how much I missed out on their lives.

"She just turned two," he says, and I hit his shoulder, just like I used to do all those years ago.

"Shut up," I say. "A doctor, a husband, and a father."

"Not the husband part," he says. "Two out of three isn't so bad." He looks at my grandfather and then back at me. "Why don't we catch up soon?" he says, and I nod at him as he walks over to his brand-new BMW.

"Doctor?" I say, shocked. "Harlow broke her arm once." I watch him drive away. "He threw up on her."

"People change," my grandfather says, and I look over at him, nodding.

"Don't I know it," I say, and he puts his hand on my shoulder.

"It's good to have you home," he says, and the guilt slowly comes back.

"It's just a visit," I say, and he nods.

"You came." He squeezes my shoulder.

"Figured it was time," I say. Someone opens the barn doors, and the horses run out into the fenced area.

I walk over to the fence and lean my hands on it. "Your father said you got hurt."

"Yeah." I don't look at him because being here with him is strange. Standing beside this man who helped make me who I am, I can't explain this feeling that creeps into me. "I'll be okay."

"So why did you come?" I can see him in my peripheral vision as he watches the horses run. "If you don't want to be here …"

"It's not that I don't want to be here, Grandpa," I say softly. "It's just …"

"Oh, I know," he says, pushing off the fence. "I know," he says softly. "Why don't you take your horse out for a bit?"

"I was going to say hi to Grandma," I say. He puts his hands in his back pockets, and I wonder if my dad ever got compared to my grandfather.

"You say hi to her when you bring back the horse and stay for dinner." He turns and starts walking to the barn. "And I'm not asking you, Reed Barnes," he says over his shoulder.

"Yes, sir," I say, walking into the fenced area and going to my horse.

He comes to me, not sure. "It's me," I say, holding out

my hand while his tail flips one way and then the other. I rub his neck. "Let's go for a ride," I say, getting onto his back without a saddle. Grabbing his reins, I kick his sides, and he starts slow. "You got lazy," I say, and he huffs back.

Eventually, he takes off a bit faster, and I enjoy the wind on my face. I don't even pay attention to where he's going, and by the time I look up, I see it. It's the red barn, but it's not red anymore, and it looks like it's falling down. I gasp out in shock as I remember how perfect it was. My eyes fixate on the barn as I remember the last night I was here.

Kissing her, tasting her, making love to her. I close my eyes, and I'm brought back to six years ago.

It had been two months since I left home. I was riding high, nothing was standing in my way, and I was making a name for myself. I opened Facebook one night and saw that I had about fifteen messages. Most of them were from my family members but one was from Hazel. Her picture was of her and her grandfather.

My heart sped up for a second when I saw her name. I opened the message.

Hey, it's me.

I know that this is out of the blue but can you call me, please.

It's important.

I deleted the app and deactivated my account that very same night. I had one goal and one goal only—to succeed. I couldn't reach out to her because I didn't trust myself not to feel the guilt. So I pushed her to the back of my mind. I put her and all the memories we had together in a nice beautiful box I never touched.

Glancing back at the house, I find it looks just as bad as the barn, and I wonder if she ever came home. I wonder if her grandfather decided to sell the farm and follow her. It wouldn't surprise me since he was all she had. I knew that her leaving was going to be a big deal to him even though he pretended he couldn't wait.

I take one last look at the barn and the house and make my way back to my grandparents' farm, not knowing that all the answers to my questions were right in front of me.

Six

Hazel

I PULL OPEN the glass door, and the cold air hits me right away. I make sure Sofia walks in before me. She slips her hand in mine as we walk in. "Good afternoon," the lady at the desk says with a smile. "How may I help you?" Her blond bob is as perfect as the makeup on her face.

"I'm here to see Mr. Devlyn," I say. "I have an appointment with him at one o'clock."

Her eyes go from smiling to sad as she gets up from her desk and walks around with her arms outstretched. "I'm so sorry about your grandfather," she says, taking me in her arms.

"Thank you," I say softly as I let her hug me.

I spent the early part of the day cleaning the downstairs

between the tears when I would find my grandfather's things. The blanket in the chair in the living room next to the bed he would cover me with when I was younger. I sat in the same chair as he did and hugged the blanket to my chest. When my phone rang at nine o'clock this morning, I was in the middle of cleaning the bathroom. It was his lawyer calling to ask me to come in. I dreaded it, but I knew I had to do it. I also knew I had no choice. Not one fucking choice.

"I'll tell Mr. Devlyn you are here." She releases me and turns to walk down the little hallway.

"Momma." I feel my hand being pulled down and look at Sofia. "Are you sad again?"

"Just a little, baby girl." I pull her to me, and my hand rubs her head.

"He's ready for you," the lady says. "If you'd like, I can keep the little one busy." She looks at Sofia. "Would you like to come and make photocopies with me?" Sofia looks up at me for permission, and I just smile and nod. "It's the first door," she tells me, taking Sofia's hand and leading her to the other side.

Walking into the office, I see the big brown desk in the middle of the room with files piled high on each side. Mr. Devlyn looks up from where he sits at his desk, getting up and taking off his glasses. He walks around the desk, with a smile, in his slacks and button-down shirt with his cuffs rolled up. He smells like tobacco and spice, something that I haven't smelled in over six years. I hold out my hand. "Mr. Devlyn."

He holds out his hand to shake, adding his other hand

over mine. “You are just as beautiful as your grandfather said you were.” I don’t say anything because a lump starts to form. I know that if I open my mouth, it’ll just be a sob coming out. “Please sit.” He points at one of the two empty chairs that face his desk.

“Thank you,” I say, sitting in a chair. My stomach feels like a boat in a tropical storm.

“Before we begin,” he starts, “I just want you to know how sorry I am for your loss.” He grabs the manila folder and opens it. “Your grandfather had everything set up.” He picks his glasses up to read the paper in front of him. “According to this, his last wish was to be cremated as soon as he passed.” I grab my purse and search for a tissue. “I want you to know that I tried to talk him out of it.” He shakes his head. “But he was a stubborn man.”

I give up searching for the tissue, and instead, I just use the back of my hand. “I’m sorry to do this,” I say. I put my trembling hand in my lap. “But I just have a couple of questions.”

“Of course.” He folds his hands in front of him. “Anything I can do to help.”

“How long was he sick?” My voice trembles.

“Two years,” he says, and I gasp in shock. “I’m taking it that you didn’t have a clue.”

“No.” I shake my head. “Not one. We saw him six months ago. I noticed he looked weak and had lost weight, but he blamed it on getting the flu.” Mr. Devlyn turns now and grabs a box of Kleenex behind him and offers me one. I grab two out of the box. “Was he alone when he passed away?” I ask the question that has haunted me since this nightmare happened.

"He wanted to do everything at home, but he got too bad to even care for him at home. He was in hospital care for the last couple of weeks," he says, and again, I'm blown away.

"We talked on FaceTime every couple of days," I say. "I mean, the last time was a week ago. But I didn't …" I shake my head, the guilt running through me. How could I not have known? How did I not notice?

"He had a strict routine. No one would be allowed in his room when you would call," he says. "I wish I had more answers for you as to why he did this, but at the end of the day, he always said that you didn't need another thing on your plate." I close my eyes, and I don't even try to stop the tears. The man who stood by my side when I found out I was pregnant. The man who didn't judge me or look at me different when I told him who the father was. The man who didn't force me to change my mind when I left his name off the birth certificate. The man who loved me so fucking unconditionally and didn't want me to be burdened. "He said you had your life out there and didn't need to come back here."

"He was one of a kind," I finally say with a little smile.

"He was," he says and looks down at his paper. "Now for the nitty-gritty stuff."

I look at him, not sure I understand. "Obviously, he left you everything that he has." I nod at him. "But his finances …" He grabs a stack of envelopes all held together by a blue rubber band. My eyes focus on that stack of papers. "His finances were not great."

"What do you mean?" I ask, confused. My grandfather always made sure everything was paid in full. It was his Southern pride that he was never late with anything. He would starve before he was late paying a bill.

"The farm had been declining in the past couple of years," he says. "He had trouble keeping up with the repairs." He takes a deep breath. "And then add the medical bills that came with him being sick."

"What are you saying?" I ask, my heart beating so fast now it's getting harder and harder to breathe.

"The house was going into foreclosure," he says. "It's obviously been stalled now since he passed away. They will give you the appropriate thirty days to make sure you put his affairs in order."

"Foreclosure," I say, not sure I heard him right over the pounding of my heart. I don't listen to the rest of what he says. When he turns and gets up, he walks around his desk and hands me the stack of envelopes.

"I will be with you every single step of the way," he says. "If you have any questions or concerns, all you have to do is call me."

I get up now, my legs a little shaky. "Thank you," I say, holding the stack of bills that now feel like they weigh a ton. "I'll let you know if I have any questions."

He walks me out, and I spot Sofia, who jumps up from the floor where she's coloring with crayons to come over to me. She stops and then turns back, going to grab the paper. "I made you a picture, Momma." She hands me the picture, and I look down at it. "It's me, you, and Pops," she says. I bend to pick her up in my arms.

"It's beautiful," I say as I turn and nod at Mr. Devlyn and his secretary, fighting back more tears. When I leave the office, the heat of the sun hits me right away. "Did you have fun?" I ask as I walk with her in my arms.

"I made photocopies of top secret work," she tells me. "Then she gave me crayons."

We stop at the grocery store before heading back home. I pick up enough food so I don't have to go out again for the next couple of days. I'm going to wait until tomorrow to tackle all these bills. Even if I wanted to do it now, my head is all over the place.

Sofia helps me carry in the groceries and stays by my side as I put away the food. It's like she knows I need her. I'm grabbing things to make dinner when there is a soft knock on the door. I look over at the door, but my feet stick on the floor like glue.

The knock comes again, and I look over at Sofia, who looks at me and then the door. I grab the rag and walk to the door. My hands shake as I unlock the door and open it just a touch. My body goes tense when I see who is standing there.

"Is that Hazel?" I hear Charlotte say, and then I'm pushed aside as Sofia sticks her face in the little opening. Charlotte gasps, and I open the door fully. She stands there holding two bags in her hands with Billy right beside her. My eyes tear up when I see him.

"Sorry," I say, trying to act as calm and cool as I can, while on the inside, I'm slightly freaking the fuck out. "Please come in," I say, moving aside and waiting for them to come in.

"We won't keep you, dear," Charlotte says, and I just smile at her.

"We heard about Kaine," Billy starts to say, and I can see the tears in his eyes. "Toughest son of a bitch I knew." Charlotte goes over to him and smiles at him. "Except for when it came to you two," he says.

"Thank you," I say and feel an arm around my leg. "Sofia," I say to her. "This is Pops' friend."

"Do you have a tractor, too?" she asks, making everyone laugh.

Billy squats down in front of her. "I do have a tractor," he says, and she smiles at him and looks up at me. "And I also have horses." Her mouth opens. "If you convince your momma to bring you over, I'll let you ride one." I don't say anything, and I thank God that neither does Sofia.

"We brought you some stuff to eat," Charlotte says, handing me the brown bags.

"You didn't have to," I say, looking at the brown bags and knowing they're filled to the brim with food. "Thank you."

"It's the least we could do," Billy says, and Charlotte just looks at him and crosses her arms over her chest. I laugh at her. "He used to come and see us," Billy starts. "Every single time he got a new picture of Sofia or when you sent him something of her, he couldn't wait to show it off." I roll my lips now as he looks at Sofia.

"We should go," Charlotte says. She comes over and takes me in her arms. "If you need anything, dear," she says, "you don't be shy."

"Thank you," I say. Billy comes to me, and when he hugs me, I close my eyes. The tears run down my face and soak into his shirt.

"You need us," he says, "you call."

He turns and waits for Charlotte to walk out before heading out the door. "Wait," I say, stepping forward. He turns now to look at me. "I have a couple of things to look through, but I was wondering if maybe you were looking to buy more property." He looks at me. "From what I was told, it's not going to be long before the bank takes it over. I know he would want you to have it."

"I'll have Casey come over with me on Monday," he says. "We'll figure it all out."

I just nod at him, and he turns and walks out of the house, closing the door softly behind him. Only then do I let go of the breath I was holding.

Seven

Reed

"WE'VE BEEN HIT." I heard the screaming all around me. "We've been hit." Opening my eyes, I was on my back. The sky above me was filled with gray clouds.

"Is everyone accounted for?" I mumbled as I tried to get enough energy to keep my eyes open. I heard a buzzing in my ear as I turned my head, feeling the blood drip off my forehead.

Shards of glass were all over me, and when I lifted my hand, it was covered in blood. "Fuckers are shooting." I heard the commotion around me as my guys tried to get to shelter.

"Cavalry is five minutes out," I heard someone say, and I dragged myself to the side of the building. Looking around, I saw the little girl in the corner. She sat with her

back to the wall, hugging her knees to her chest. She held out her hand to me with tears streaming down her face.

"Cover me," I said, trying to get up, but the guys wanted to stop me. I took one step toward the little girl before I heard the click, and everything blew up.

My eyes fly open, and I see the darkness again. I raise my hand to my face and see that it's clean. My chest heaves, and I make it just in time to vomit in the trash can by the bed.

I climb out of bed, walking to the bathroom. My body and head feel numb from reliving the dream over and over again. After rinsing out my mouth, I slip on shorts and walk to the kitchen to make coffee. Seeing it's a little after five in the morning, I grab my coffee, walk outside, and sit down, looking ahead.

Sunday is the day I finally get to see everyone. I mean, I've seen a couple of people since I've been back, but mostly, they've been giving me my space. Grabbing my running shoes, I walk over to the gym and get on the treadmill, replaying what I did yesterday to bring on the nightmare. I was going on two days without having that fucking dream, so the only thing I can think of is that I didn't work out hard enough.

I run on the treadmill for a couple of hours. My head goes over lists and lists of things for me to do. It also comes up with excuses for me to leave early.

When I get dressed later, in jeans and a white shirt, I decide to walk to my grandparents' house. Prolonging the inevitable, I can see the people as soon as I get closer. It never fails, and for the first time since I've been here,

I actually smile. I spot a couple of kids running toward me and see Ethan's son, Gabriel, with Tucker, Chelsea's son. "Hey, Uncle Reed," Gabriel says. "My dad said you would be later because he pushed you so hard yesterday that you wouldn't be able to walk."

I grab Gabriel around his neck, teasing him. "Is that so?" I joke with him and pick him up. The sound of him laughing gets me.

I put him down and bend to pick up Tucker, who I've met through fucking FaceTime. "You look like your dad," I say, and he smiles.

"I'm going to be strong like him," he says, and I laugh. I walk with my arms around Gabriel and Tucker all the way to the chaos that is my family.

"This one yours?" I look at Ethan, and he smirks.

"He talks a big game." I look at him. "You need to bring him into the gym," I say.

"Nah," Ethan says. "He's too busy trying to be a cowboy."

"Really?" I look over at him, and he smiles big. "You don't say."

"I'm going to be rodeo king," he says proudly.

"You think so," I say, and he nods his head and crosses his arms over his chest very much like his father. "Well, I'll stop by this week and see what you got."

"Uncle Reed." I hear my father talking and look over at him. "He was the best cowboy I've ever seen." Gabriel looks at me like he's unsure. "If he stayed with it, I have no doubt he would have destroyed my record."

"That's not exactly true," I say, and he looks at me.

"Yes, it is. You were twelve years old and walked out after the best round anyone has ever seen and you were, like, done. Nothing could change your mind," he says, and I have to shake my head. The memory is now a little bit foggy.

"There you are," I hear Chelsea say, coming to us. "I have been looking for you all over the place."

"Is she talking to you or me?" I ask Tucker, who shrugs.

"I'm talking to both of you." She comes over and gives me a hug first. "Asshole," she whispers so no one can hear and then stands back and punches me in my shoulder.

"Mom," Tucker says, laughing.

"That's for not calling me back," she says and then punches me again. "That's for not coming home in six years." She pulls her hand back again, but Mayson grabs her around her waist.

"Easy there," he says, putting his hand on her stomach. "Leave the man be."

"Yeah." I place Tucker in front of me holding him as a shield, in case she tries to hit me again. "Leave me be."

"Auntie Savannah," I call to my aunt, who is sitting with my mother. She gets up and rushes over to me.

"You little shit," she says softly as she puts her head on my chest. "You're too skinny," she says, and I laugh now.

"Chelsea hit me," I say, putting an arm around her shoulder, and she shakes her head. "Twice." I hold up two fingers. "Tell her, Tucker."

"Don't you," Chelsea says to her son, and he laughs at her. I'm about to say something else when I see my brother, Quinn, walking in. His little girl, Grace, is on his hip as she looks up at him and tells him something. Willow is walking beside them.

Quinn looks around the yard, and when he spots me, he points in my direction, and she smiles. Another kid I met through FaceTime. He walks over to us. "Here he is. Uncle Reed," he says, and I scrunch my nose up to her.

I hold out my hands to her, and to my surprise, she comes to me. "Want to go pet the horses?" I ask, and she nods.

"Where is Amelia?" Chelsea asks, looking around, and I see her waddling in.

"She looks pissed," I say and then look back at the group. "Why does she look so pissed?"

"She's almost overdue," Chelsea says, laughing, but then turns her face when Amelia glares at us.

"She should blame her husband," I tell the group. "He put her in that state." I look back down at Grace. "Let's get away before she comes over."

"She needs to wash her hands," Willow says, "before she eats."

"She's fine," Quinn says. "Reed has her."

I turn now and kiss Grace's head. "When did you get so big?" I ask, and she points with her finger.

"Horse," she says, and I laugh.

When we get to the barn, I put her down and hold out my hand. "Ready, girl?" She nods her head and walks with me. "Show me where your horse is," I say. She pulls my hand toward her stall, and sure enough, her name is out there.

She doesn't stop talking for five seconds, and when my father comes into the barn an hour later, she runs to him. "Grampy," she says. "Uncle Reed said a bad word."

"One time," I tell my father. "You weren't supposed to tell anyone." I walk to her and tickle her stomach. She tries to push me off through her giggles.

"It's good to have you home," my father says with a smile on his face.

"Yeah, it's nice." I surprise even myself when I admit it as I follow him out of the barn.

Kids are running around everywhere, and I see Christopher talking with Harlow. "Feels just like it always did." I laugh now. "Except another generation."

"It's amazing to see," my father says. "When Dad started this tradition, it was only Ethan."

"Now there are five hundred of us," I joke. My father puts Grace down and holds her hand.

"I heard you pushed it in the gym," he says, and I nod.

"Yeah, it's been good," I say. "I have an appointment on Tuesday with the same doctor Ethan used to talk to."

"He's good," my father says, and I nod. My father played a big part in Ethan coming back home. "Came highly recommended back then, so I can only imagine now."

"I have about three more weeks," I say, and he smiles, and then you see the sadness in his eyes.

"I missed you," he says softly.

"We spoke all the time," I say, the guilt starting to

creep over me now.

"I know," he says, and Grace lets go of his hand. "Go see Grammy," he tells Grace, and we watch her walk toward my mom. "But having you here," he says, "I just realized how much I missed you." He puts his hand around my neck like I did to Gabriel not long ago. "Even your shitty attitude."

I laugh. "I never had a shitty attitude," I say, and his hand comes up to slap his stomach as he bursts out howling with laughter.

"It was close," he says. "I thought I was going to have to knock you out at one point." I look over at him. "You need to thank your mother and your grandfather for saving your life."

I shake my head. "You didn't even know you were being a little shit." My father looks at me. "You were miserable, completely and utterly miserable, and the minute you told us you were leaving, you were a changed person."

"I didn't know that you knew," I say softly, feeling bad about the way I acted without even knowing. "I thought I hid it."

"Maybe to the people who didn't know you or have to live with you," my father says. "But to anyone who knew you." He shakes his head. "It was your grandfather who called it." My eyebrows pinch together. "'Set him free,'" he told me. "He'll come back." My father looks toward Quinn and Harlow, who laugh at something. "The hardest thing in my life was having you leave, knowing in my heart you would never come back." I see the tears form in his eyes. “Keeping strong in front of your mother was the second hardest thing.” He smirks, turning and slapping his hand on my shoulder. “You’ll never understand until you have a child,” he says. I want to hold up my hand and tell him that it will never happen. “Why don’t you do your dad a favor,” he says, “and come spend the day with me tomorrow?”

Seeing my father so open with me shifts something inside me, knowing he knew how unhappy I was and that he struggled with it just as much as I did. *Today is a good day*, I think to myself. Today, for the first time in six years, I’m happy to be here. I say the word that shocks both of us, not knowing just how much my life is going to change. “Okay.”

Eight

Hazel

THE SMELL OF lemon fills the air as I pass the hardwood floor in the living room. "Okay," I say, walking back to the pails and rinsing it off once. I wash it one more time before I think it's clean enough. The soft breeze from outside comes into the house. For the past two days, I've been cleaning the house from top to bottom. I was doing everything I needed to in order to keep myself from breaking down, but I was starting to wear thin. The days are filled with cleaning the house, and the nights are filled with regret and questions. I start angry and then slowly end up with my head on the kitchen table while I sob. My grandfather is gone, and now I have to give up the only thing I have left of him.

Billy showing up is a sign. If anyone out there was

willing to buy the farm, it would be the Barneses. It's no secret that they own most of the properties, so what's one more?

Asking Billy to buy the farm was a huge thing. Now that I knew Casey would be coming around, my nerves were on edge. I'm barely sleeping, and when I do, all I do is dream of Reed, which makes me wake up in a pissed-off mood. "Why don't we start moving the furniture?" I look at Sofia, who is wearing jean overalls with rubber boots.

The company just came by and picked up Pops' hospital bed. "Where do you want to put this?" Sofia points at the recliner where Pops used to sit.

"That," I say with a smile on my face. "Goes right here." I push it to the spot in the corner where it always was. "You know why?" She shakes her head. "Because you can see who comes to the front door," I say, pointing at the window and seeing that it is true, but now with the overgrown weeds, you can't see anything really. "And you see the television perfect." She nods her head at me, and I push the stuff around. The hair on the top of my head is slowly falling out of the bun. It takes me over an hour of pushing to fix things. The whole time, Sofia is either sitting and watching or "helping."

"There," I say, pushing the couch against the wall. "How's this?" I look over at Sofia, who is helping by pushing her side of the couch.

"I like it," she says, plopping down on the couch. "Comfy." She pats the space next to her. "Come sit, Momma."

"Okay." I smile as I sit next to her, putting my arm around her and pulling her to me. I kiss her soft brown hair. "Much better," I say, looking down at her. "You make everything better, Sofia." The ding of the kitchen timer rings, letting me know my cookies are ready.

Sofia flies off the couch and jumps up and down. "It's ready." She puts her hands together with excitement.

"They are," I say, getting up and walking to the kitchen.

"Be careful, Momma," she tells me. "It's hot."

I laugh at her and grab the oven mitt, opening the oven. The two baking trays are on the middle rack, and the cookies are a golden brown. "They look good," I tell Sofia, putting them on the stovetop. She comes over to stand next to me, not getting too close, and gets on her tippy-toes. Ever since I had Sofia, baking has been my favorite pastime. I had a book of recipes from my great-grandmother that Pops brought me when he visited once Sofia was born. Batch after batch, I would give it my own spin. It even helped out when things were tight, and I would sell the cookies at school. Word spread, and it was a quick side job, but I've not done this in a while. The only cookies I bake now are for Sofia's school and us.

"Can I have one?" she asks.

"Soon," I say, and she yawns. "Are you tired?" She shakes her head and rubs her eyes. She woke up at four thirty today and refused to go back to sleep.

"Why don't we go and snuggle and watch a movie, and then we can have some cookies and milk?" I pick her up, and she puts her head on my shoulder.

Walking up the stairs, I pass my grandfather's room. The door is closed, but I know I'm going to have to open it sooner rather than later. The floor creaks when I walk into my bedroom. I set Sofia on the bed and take off her boots, and she crawls to the middle of the bed. The iPad sits on my dresser, and I use it to find one of her shows. I press play, and by the time I lie down next to her, she's already asleep. Grabbing my old blanket, I cover her and softly kiss her cheek.

I leave the iPad playing and sneak out of the room as quietly as I can, turning back and looking at her every single time the floor creaks to make sure she stays asleep. I pull the door but leave it open just a touch.

Walking down the steps, I make my way to the kitchen, grabbing the kettle and putting it on the burner. Turning the knob, I listen for the click of the gas stove. I get my cup out and put a tea bag in it.

Looking over at the table, I have my laptop and the stack of bills that Mr. Devlyn gave me when I left. The kettle whistles, and I pour the boiling water into the mug, suddenly wishing I bought a bottle of wine or maybe two when we were out.

Sitting down, I place the tea in front of me and let out a huge breath. Pulling the blue elastic off the stack of letters, I open the first bill, and my eyes go from the top where the supplier name is to the red "past due" stamped in the middle to the bottom where the amount is. I repeat the process until the stack is all opened.

My head is spinning now when I see how much is

owed. The biggest one from the hospital and then the hospice care. I close my eyes when I get to the bank one. Not only did he take a mortgage out on the house but he also took a second mortgage on that one.

Opening my laptop, I start entering things, and my head is spinning as I think about how the fuck I'm going to make it out of this debt. Not even sure selling the farm will cover it.

The sound of a truck door closing has me looking up, and my heart's starting to beat faster and faster when I hear a soft knock on the door. *This is it,* I think to myself and look down. My blue jeans fit like a glove, which surprised me since they were from high school, and I have that on with a button-down plaid shirt. If you didn't know any better, you would think I lived here full-time.

I take a deep breath and turn the lock on the door and open it. Casey is standing at the bottom of the porch now, and he's looking down. He looks up when he hears the door open. "Hey," he says, and I swallow and wonder if he can tell I'm nervous.

Knowing I was coming here was one thing, but seeing Reed's family was a whole different ball game. "Hi." I smile back at him and walk out of the house, closing the door behind me. "Billy said you would be …" I start to say, and then the world crashes around me. The passenger door opens, and I have to hold the doorframe when I see him. The man who changed my life without so much as a second thought. The man who gave me the best gift I've ever received in my life, then broke my heart. I lean back on the door for support as I look at him. I always thought

I would see him again one day. This scenario played over and over in my head over the years, but none of them were like this. None of them were here on the same farm that it ended just as soon as it started. No, in my head, I would be dressed up, and he would be sorry, not me in my old high school clothes.

"Holy shit," Reed says, smiling, and I take him in. Everything inside me goes stiff as my head screams out. All the images I had in my head were wrong. They were of a different person because the person standing in front of me isn't him. He's bigger, much bigger. His hair looks the same, and when he puts his glasses on his head, his eyes are more dangerous than the last time I looked into them. "I didn't know you would be here." He puts his hands on his hips, which makes his arms even bigger.

There is so much I want to say to him, and none of it good, but right now, I just need him gone. The thought of Sofia getting up and walking outside is too much for me to handle. My knees are literally one second away from giving out. My mouth is so dry, and the heat from the sun is making me feel like I'm going to have heatstroke. Focus, my head tells me. Yes, just focus. "Here I am," I say, my tone tight. I look back at Casey, who is standing there looking at me. "Billy said you would be passing by."

I can feel Reed staring at me and feel the pull to look back at him. "I'm sorry about your grandfather," Casey says, and I just nod at him. "Before I even offer you anything, would it be okay if we took a look around?"

"That's fine," I say. "I don't know how safe the barn

is. We …" I stop myself. "I was going in there yesterday, and a family of raccoons chased me out," I say, and Casey smiles at me.

"Since when are you afraid of raccoons?" Reed asks, and I just look over at him.

"Things change." I look back at Casey, and he looks from me to Reed, then back over at me. I've never really had a conversation with him. Usually, it was just a hello in passing or taking his glass from him at the bar when I worked there.

"I'll take a look around and come back over tomorrow. We can sit down then and see what we can do."

"Okay," I say, turning and opening the door. I step inside without even saying goodbye. My heart hammers in my chest, and I close the door and slowly sink to the floor. "This is not good," I say, looking over at the window when I hear them walk around. "This is not good at all."

Nine

Reed

THE DOOR CLOSES behind her, and I look over at my father, who just shakes his head. "What the hell was that?" I ask, pointing at the door.

"Son …" He tries not to laugh. "I've been with your mother for over twenty years. I've gotten many looks in that time, but that"—he points at the door—"was a woman who is pissed. And I know a pissed-off woman when I see one." I open my mouth and then close it. "I don't know what you did to her, but if she had a gun, she would have put a bullet in your foot."

"I've been gone for six years." My hands are still on my hips, and my feet are glued to the ground. I stay here waiting for her to open the door and come back out and be like, just kidding. I look at my father, who starts walking toward the barn, and back at the door that she just slammed in my face.

"What the fuck?" I follow my father. "Jesus," I say when I have to make my way through the weeds. "This is bad," I say, looking at my father, and he nods. "Kaine never had his property like this." I take a look around and then back at the house. Weeds as tall as me are along the back porch. The back porch that looks like it's going to fall off the house. I look into the windows, hoping to see her one more time.

"It got bad last year," my father starts. "Grandpa and I came by and did his grass when he was out." I listen. "Then he called and told me if I stepped on his property again, he would shoot me."

"Well, then, maybe that's why she was pissed," I say, looking down to make sure there are no snakes.

"She was pissed at you," my father reminds me. "She smiled at me."

We get close to the barn, and my heart speeds up again. My father goes into the barn through the open door, and I gasp. It was so clean six years ago, and now it's dusty. The only thing still in the barn in the corner is his tractor. I look up at the loft where I spent the night with Hazel and see that the ladder has been removed. Half the roof has rotted through, too. "This thing needs to be demolished," my father says, looking around. "Let's get out of here before someone gets hurt."

I walk out now and stand with my father. "It's a lot of land," I say, looking far off into the distance where I know his land ends.

"It is," my father says, turning to walk back to his truck. After getting in the truck, I take one look back at the house, my eyes going to the window that I know is her bedroom. When we drive away, I close my eyes.

When my father asked me to come to work with him, I thought we would be in the clubhouse doing office work or even at the riding track. What I was not expecting was to be touring farms. The minute he turned into the road to the house, my heart sped up.

"What are we doing here?" I asked, looking at the trees as we drove closer and closer to Hazel's house.

"I told Grandpa I would pass by here," he told me, and I thought nothing of it. "Kaine passed away a couple of days ago," he said, and my head whipped around so fast I thought I was going to get whiplash. My only thought was that Hazel must be devastated. He hung the moon and the stars according to her, and she was his everything.

He got out of the truck, and I sat in the passenger seat, my leg bouncing up and down. My eyes took in the house, and I remembered Hazel as if she were right in front of me. Then the door opened, and she was. I was shocked. My hand came out and opened the door before I even knew what was happening.

I looked at her, and I swear on my life, my heart did a fucking flip at the same time my stomach sank and then rose again. My heart was going like a jackhammer, and there was nothing I could have done to stop it. She was so fucking gorgeous I couldn't stop the smile from coming to my face. Her hair was tied up on top of her head, and her jeans hugged her just like they did all those years ago. Trust me, I know. I spent a good month working side by side with her, carrying one of the gray plastic buckets to hide the hard-on I had for her.

"Why are you so quiet?" my father asks, and I turn back, playing that scene over and over again in my mind.

"Just thinking," I say as he pulls up at my grandparents' house.

He doesn't push me as he gets out of the truck, and I follow him into the house. The smell of baking hits me right away as I make my way to the kitchen, where my grandmother is standing with fresh baked muffins in front of her. "Hey, Grandma," I say, walking and bending to kiss her cheek.

"Don't 'hey, Grandma' me." She moves out of my touch. "That didn't work when you were fifteen, and it's not going to work now. Go wash your hands, and then you can have one," she says, and my father laughs. "You, too," she says. I turn around and laugh at him, pointing.

"Your mom just schooled you," I say, walking to the sink where he joins me and pushes me, making me laugh more.

"Where is Dad?" my father asks, grabbing the rag and drying his hands, and then grabbing a muffin.

"He's …" she starts to say, but the back door opens, and he walks in. "There he is." She looks at us. "Did you guys eat?"

"Yeah," my father answers. "But I'll have another muffin."

I grab one and walk over to the table to sit down. My

grandfather walks to my grandmother and kisses her on the lips. “Love you,” he says to her, and she looks up at him with all the love in the world.

“I’m eating,” my father says, groaning.

“Now you know how I feel,” I say. “Imagine if he grabbed her butt.” My grandparents laugh while my father glares. “Scared. I was scared for my life.” My grandfather walks over to the sink and washes his hands, knowing the wrath he will suffer if he doesn’t.

“Shut up,” my father says, shaking his head.

My grandfather takes off his hat and comes to sit at the table with me. “You went to work?” he asks, and I nod. “Obviously not hard work,” he says. “Your shirt is still white.” He snickers while my grandmother puts a plate of cookies and muffins on the table. “Come work with me.”

“He won’t survive,” my father says, pulling out the empty chair beside me.

“Are you kidding me?” I shake my head. “I spent the night in the ocean, in the rain.”

My grandfather chuckles as my grandmother brings him a drink. She stands next to him and puts her arm around his shoulders. He smiles up at her and puts his hand around her waist. “Did you go by Kaine’s?” my grandfather asks, and my father just nods.

“Yeah, just came from there,” he says.

“And what do you think?” He picks up his drink and takes a sip, bringing his other hand onto the table.

“I think that …” He shakes his head. “We are going to lose money as soon as we pay off his debt.”

I look over at my father, not sure what he's talking about. "Kaine has no debt," I say.

"Stubborn, stubborn man," my grandfather says. "Always was." He laughs. "It's why we got along so well."

"He has more debt than the land will cover. The barn needs to be demolished. The house looks like it's had better days," my father says.

"Well," my grandfather says, "we take a loss." He leans back in his chair. "I know he would do it for me. And there is no way in hell I'm going to let Hazel and her little girl get shorted in all this."

My head snaps back, not sure I heard right. "Little girl?" I ask, confused. "She has a daughter?"

"Yeah," my grandfather says, "met her the other day when we went by there." My mouth suddenly goes dry. He smiles. "Chip off the old block. Looks just like her. Sweet as hell, asked me about a tractor."

"Holy shit," I say, not realizing I'm saying the words out loud until my grandmother smacks my shoulder. "Sorry, Grandma." My head is spinning. She's a mom. She is probably here with her husband, and I was thinking about her with a semi boner. I have so many questions, but all I can think of is she has a kid. "A kid," I say out loud.

"The only thing in the world Kaine loved was Hazel and her little girl. Even if he didn't want to ask for it, the only thing he would care about is for Hazel and Sofia to be taken care of," my grandfather says, and I repeat Sofia in my head.

"We can't just show up there and pay off the debt," my father says, and my grandfather nods.

"No way," he says. "Not if she's anything like Kaine."

"She's stubborn as hell," I put in. My grandparents look at me in shock while my father laughs at me.

"She ignored him," my father says with great pride, and I glare at him yet again.

"Reed Barnes," my grandmother says, putting her hands on her hips. "If you were rude to her …"

I hold my hands up. "I didn't say anything to her." *This time*, but I don't add that in.

"So, what do you want to do?" my father asks, and even I know the answer to this one.

"We buy it from her and make sure she has some extra for her and her daughter," my grandmother says, and my grandfather nods. "If you need money, I have it."

"I don't need your money, Mom," my father says. "Okay, I have to go back tomorrow. I'll take a look and see if I can find all the outstanding bills Kaine owes."

"Isn't that illegal?" I ask, and it's his turn to glare at me.

"If it's on the internet, it's not illegal." He gets up now, kissing his mother and then turning toward me. "Find a way home." He turns and walks out of the house.

I wait for the door to close behind my father before I look back at my grandparents. My grandmother sits down. "I don't know how she's going to do it." She shakes her head. "It's bad enough raising a child as a single mom, but to do it without family." I take in the part where she's single. "And they were so close." She grabs a tissue and wipes the corner of her eyes.

"I thought she left to go to college," I say. "Didn't know she came back home."

"She doesn't live here," my grandfather says. "First time she's been back in six years."

I look at him as all the questions come at me at once. "She was probably embarrassed," my grandmother says. "Getting pregnant in college." My mouth hangs open. "And then having a baby alone. That would be hard on anyone."

I get up, ready to jump out of my skin. "I'm going to go," I say. "I have to meet Ethan," I lie to them. "See you tomorrow."

Walking out of the house, I walk toward the house I'm staying at, the whole time wondering what the fuck Hazel has been up to.

Ten

Hazel

"TILT YOUR HEAD back," I tell my daughter as I grab a plastic cup and rinse the shampoo out of her hair.

"Momma," she says. "My eyes." I grab a clean, dry towel and dry the little drops of water running down the side of her face. "Thank you, Momma," she says with a smile, and it knocks me on my ass because she has his smile. I never saw it before, or maybe I didn't want to see it before, but the way she smirks and then smiles, she's exactly like him. Seeing him again and then seeing some of the stuff she does, it's like I forgot or ignored it. But now seeing him and knowing that he's so close to her, it's almost like they stick out more. It's not just her smile either. It's the way she puts her hands on her hips and cocks her head to one side just a bit.

"Five more minutes," I say, and she turns around in a circle in the big tub. "We have a big day tomorrow," I say. Sitting on the wooden stool by the tub, I watch her fill the cup with water and then throw it on her legs. "We are going to take care of those weeds out front." She looks up at me. "Cut them down. Pops always loved his flowers in the front. It's because Meemaw planted them." I take a big inhale when I think of what I need to do in order to make it look a bit better. "We just need to go into the barn."

Her eyes get big now. "Momma, the raccoons," she tells me. "They looked mad last time."

"It's fine." I'm not sure it's fine, but they're not going to stop me. I need the tools in the barn because without them, I'll be cutting the weeds with the scissors. "Momma will bring out a big pot and a wooden spoon, and we'll scare them all away." She looks at me like she isn't sure, and it doesn't help that I think she's right.

She stands, saying, "Okay, I'm done." I hold out my hand for her as she climbs out of the old tub. She stands on the little square rug while I pick up the big dry towel on my lap and wrap it around her. Pulling her to me, I squish her to my chest, blowing kisses in her neck until the sound of her giggles fills the room. "Momma, that tickles," she says, and I finally dry her off so she can slip on her nightgown. I start combing her hair to braid it. "Momma, can I have a cookie?"

"One cookie, some milk, and then bed," I say, and she smirks at me, the same fucking smirk that Reed gave me when he was over. The smirk I forgot about until today.

"Okay," she sings, knowing I'll give her two cookies.

We walk back downstairs to the soft light coming from the kitchen stove. She sits on the chair on her knees while she eats two cookies and then drinks her milk. "Let's go brush your teeth," I say, walking upstairs to finish her nightly routine. I'm trying to keep the same schedule for her.

After she brushes her teeth, she jumps into the bed and slips under the covers. "Prayers," she says, and I sit on the bed beside her. She takes her arms out of the covers and folds her hands, closing her eyes. "Now I lay me down to sleep." Her soft voice fills the room. The same room that I used to say these exact prayers. "God bless Mommy and Pops." I smile at her. "And all my friends." I bend down and kiss her nose.

"Good night, sweet girl," I say, and she turns. "Have colorful dreams."

Standing, I walk out of the room and pull the door closed just a touch. I clean up the bathroom before walking back downstairs and turning on the kettle. Walking over to the kitchen table, I open my laptop, getting all the papers ready to go over again.

I've been over it five times, and I still can't figure out how the fuck I'm going to get out of this mess. The only thing that will help is if Billy buys the farm.

The sound of the kettle whistling fills the room. I pick up the kettle and pour out the hot water, and I'm suddenly brought back to six years ago.

I walked into the house after discovering I was pregnant. The television was on low, and Pops' chair was empty. I walked into the kitchen, and there he stood, making his nightly tea. He looked over his shoulder, and the smile he had on his face quickly dropped when he saw my face. He put the kettle down and turned to look at me. He was wearing his jeans and flannel shirt with his suspenders that he always wore. "What in sam hill has you in that mood?"

My heart beat so fast I thought it would come out of my chest. My stomach was moving like a lost boat in the ocean during a storm. "I have to tell you something."

"Well, go on, then," he said, his voice tight as he waited to hear.

"I'm," I started to talk, and my voice trembled. "I'm," I started over again, and that time the tears stopped me from talking. His eyes remained on mine the whole time; his face pure white as he held the counter.

He stood at six foot four and was built like an ox, but he was as soft as a teddy bear. "Hazel Bernadette." He said my full name, and I knew he was one second from snapping.

"I'm pregnant." The words left my mouth without a second thought. I watched his hand come up to his chest, and I thought he was having a heart attack.

"Jesus, Mary, and Joseph." He laughed. "I thought you were going to tell me you were dying." He grabbed his tea and walked over to the table and sat down. He looked at me and then at the empty chair beside him. That was my cue to get my ass in the chair. I pulled out the chair and was suddenly thankful to be sitting down while I was doing this. "Now ..." He looked at me. "Start

over."

I placed my hands on the table, and my eyes focused on my fingers instead of Pops because I wasn't sure I could see the disappointment in his eyes. "I'm pregnant," I said softly, still in shock myself. How did this happen? *I kept asking myself that over and over since I saw the two lines. We used protection both times.*

"So whatcha going to do?" he asked, and I finally looked up at him. Nothing was in his eyes but love.

"I'm going to have the baby," I said, and he nodded.

"It ain't going to be easy." He placed his hand on mine now. "But if anyone can do it." Tears filled his eyes now. "You can."

"I don't know about that," I said. "I never expected this."

"No one does really." He grabbed his cup now and brought it to his mouth. "Even when you know it's coming." He placed the cup back down. "What about the father?"

I shook my head. "He doesn't know," I answered him honestly.

"Are you going to let him know?" The question lingered in the air.

"He left town," I said, and without saying Reed's name, he knew. "So I don't know."

"He's got a big family," he said. "One of them might know how to get ahold of him."

"I'll try," I told him and then looked at him. "Are you disappointed in me?"

He put his big hand back on mine and squeezed as

tears filled his eyes. "Not in a million years. Couldn't be more proud of you." He took his handkerchief out of his pocket and dabbed his eyes. "In my whole life, you are the only thing I am most proud of." I got up and kissed his cheek. "Now go try to get ahold of that man of yours."

I stood there in front of him with tears rolling down my face. "What if he doesn't want the baby?" Reed couldn't wait to get the hell out of town, so the last thing he would want is a child.

"Then he's a damn fool," he said as he got up. "And it'll be his loss. We'll figure it out."

I sit at the table now. "We'll figure it out," I say to the empty room. "We always do." I smile, ignoring the pain in my chest. He made sure I was always okay. He made sure we were always okay.

I'm going over the bills again when I hear the soft knock. The paper in my hand doesn't move because I thought I might have been hearing things. I look over at the front door when I hear it again, and my hand slowly lowers to the table. I think about ignoring it for a second, but then the knocking starts again.

I walk softly to the door, and the knock sounds again. "Fucking hell." I look upstairs and see that she is still asleep. I unlock the door and pull it open. I knew he would come back. I knew it, yet I was in denial.

"Hey, Hazel." He stands where his father stood this morning. "You busy?"

I step out and pull the door closed behind me. "What do you want, Reed?" In the dark of the outside, I can't see his eyes.

"I thought, you know, we could catch up," he says, and I fold my arms over my chest.

"Did you?" I ask, rolling my eyes. I really hope he can see how fucking annoyed I am that he's here. The last thing I want to do is catch up with Reed Barnes. What he needs to do is be on his way and pretend he didn't see me.

"What's it been now?" He mirrors my stance and folds his arms over his chest. "Six years."

"I don't know. I'm not keeping track." I shake my head. "If that's all," I say, turning and putting my hand on the door handle.

"So you're a mom?" His words have me stopping in my tracks and ice goes through my veins. I close my eyes, and I'm happy that my back is to him so he can't see how shaken I am. "Yeah, I was over at my grandparents', and my grandfather said he met your little girl." My heart is beating so fast and so fucking hard I don't think I can even handle turning around. "Sofia," he says her name. "Said she looks just like her momma."

I turn now to face him, anger filling my whole body. He doesn't get to do this. He does not get to come in here and claim her after not even bothering to answer me. She's mine, and she will always be mine. "She does," I say. "She looks just like me. So if that's it, Reed, I have other things to do." I turn around this time, ready to go back into the house and hoping like hell he just lets it go.

Eleven

REED

"WHY ARE YOU so pissed?" I ask, and for the second time tonight, she stops in her tracks and turns back to glare at me.

I sat at home the whole night, wondering if I should come see her or just leave it. After talking myself out of going to her, something big pushed me to get off my ass and walk over to her house. The house was pitch black with just a small light coming from the kitchen. I thought about throwing some pebbles at her window like old times, but I didn't know where she would be in the house. I also didn't know if she was in that room or if it was Sofia's, so I knocked on the door. I was about to give up when she came out, closing the door behind her, and I hated that I couldn't see her face properly. The only light I had was from the moon, and it didn't do her justice. Nothing could.

"I'm not pissed," she huffs out. "I'm busy dealing with stuff I can't control. I don't have time to go down memory lane with you." I want her to tell me all the things she needs to do. I want her to tell me what I missed in six years. "Good night, Reed," she says, ending the conversation, and I finally let her walk back into her house. I wait until I hear the sound of the lock before I hang my head.

"Well, that didn't go as planned," I tell myself and turn to walk back to my house. The sound of an owl hooting fills the darkness. The ground crunches and snaps under my boots as I walk in the forest, replaying the whole conversation with her in my head. I knew that she had a full plate. Seeing the debt Kaine left her and then seeing what the land was worth, it didn't take a rocket scientist to see she was up shit creek without a paddle. I also knew there was no way I would let her sink. I didn't give a shit how pissed she was at me. She saved me all those years ago when I thought I would drown. Those last couple of months were the worst, and I got the escape I needed with her. I told her my deepest darkest secrets, and not once did she judge me. Not once did she look at me like I was crazy. Not once did she see anyone but me. All of me.

Walking up the back porch, I open the door and head straight to the bottle of whiskey. Taking it out, I pour a shot and put it on the counter, turning and getting my laptop. I'm going to go down memory lane, and I might need help doing it. I sit at the counter and wait for it to boot up.

My leg moves up and down as I wait. It may take just a couple of minutes, but to me, it's the longest fucking time in the world. Opening the browser, I type Facebook and wait for the page to load. I add in my email address and the password to access my account. I spot Harlow right away on my news feed. Looking up at the red numbers staring at me, one says nine hundred and ninety-nine with a plus sign, and the inbox shows me six hundred and ninety-five messages.

I don't bother scrolling. Instead, I open my messages and then look at the shot of whiskey. My stomach is a fucking mess. I go down one at a time, ignoring all of them, and wonder if it would even be there six years later. Maybe messages are deleted after a certain time, but then I see her name—Hazel.

I click to open the message, but her picture doesn't show up. Instead, it's just an outline of a person. I see her message there, and my stomach burns just like it did all those years ago. It was the worst day of training. I had woken up and felt like I was missing something or someone, and I just couldn't shake it. I ignored it all day long, only to have it hit me again when I was in the shower. I closed my eyes, and all I saw was my family. My mother and father sitting at the table laughing. My grandfather on his horse, and Hazel laughing with her head back and her hair blowing in the wind.

I read the message and then deactivated my account. I thought about answering, but I knew if I did, I would just string her along, and she deserved better.

My hands touch the keyboard when I type Hey and press enter. As soon as I do it, a red exclamation mark appears. "What the fuck does this mean?" I put the mouse cursor next to the red dot and see the mark of error. I enter another message, and the same thing happens. I go back to my home page and type out her name in the search bar. The five people who come up I don't even know. "What the fuck?" I grab my phone and call Harlow.

"What's up, big brother?" she says, answering right away.

"Hey, can you give me your Facebook login?" I ask, signing out of my account.

"Um, no," she says right away. "Why would you want my login? Use your own." I close my eyes and pinch the bridge of my nose. Of course it wouldn't be this easy.

"Fine, bye," I say, hanging up the phone and calling my mother.

"She's not going to give you her login," Harlow says, picking up my mother's cell phone.

"Why do you still live at home?" I ask. "Isn't it the time you left home?"

"I just ate dinner. And now I'm lying on the couch. Know who cooked me dinner?" she says. "Mom. Now I'm going to go and soak in the tub that the cleaning lady cleaned today."

"You are a spoiled brat," I say. "Now, can I speak to my mother, please?" I say, shaking my head.

"Well, you can't. She and Dad went out on a date," she says. "And she forgot her phone."

“Fine, thanks.” I hang up and think about calling my father, but I don’t want to interrupt them on their date.

Instead, I shut down the computer. Tomorrow I’ll go back and ask her what she wanted to tell me all those years ago. Tomorrow.

I lie in bed most of the night, sleep not coming to me. The last time I see the clock, it’s a little past three o’clock in the morning. The knocking wakes me up, and it takes me a second to come to realize what the noise is when the knocking comes again. I get out of bed and run to the door when the knocking continues. “Hold your horses!” I shout. Unlocking the door, I see Ethan standing there with his hands on his hips and his glasses on.

“Good afternoon,” he says, pushing me and coming into the house.

“What time is it?” I ask, confused.

“Nine thirty,” he says, and I stare at him in shock. “Jesus, why didn’t my alarm wake me?” I walk back into the house, going to the kitchen to see my phone on the counter. “I must have been in a deep sleep not to hear my alarm.”

He slaps me on the back. “Means your body needed the rest.” He sits on the stool while I make some coffee. “You have to learn to listen to your body.”

“Give me five minutes,” I say. “I’ll be ready to go then.” I grab the coffee and then go get dressed.

I push myself in the gym. My whole body burns when I walk out and head back home for a shower. That night, I get into the truck, and my vehicle leads me to drive by Hazel’s place. The lights are out again, and I stop the truck and think about ringing the bell again. But instead, I press the gas and make my way over to the bar.

After parking and getting out, it feels like I just did this yesterday. I pull open the door and step inside, looking around at the bigger space. The back goes far back, and to the side, what used to be the sports bar is now open. I head to the bar, and I stop when I see Harlow behind the bar. She looks up and smiles when she sees me. "Holy, holy," I say when I see her behind the bar, and she just shakes her head. I look in front of her and see Christopher and clap my hands together. "Talk about bringing back memories." I walk over and slap his back as I sit down next to him.

"This is crazy," Christopher says, bringing the bottle of beer to his mouth. "Never did we sit on this side of the bar."

"Didn't think I would see you here," I say honestly.

"On the one day a week I get off, I decided that I deserved to have a cold beer served to me by a beautiful woman," he says, looking over at Harlow.

"That's still my sister." I glare at him. "Which means she's off-limits."

"What can I get you?" Harlow interrupts us with a huge smile on her face.

"What are you doing here?" I ask, and she walks to get me a beer.

"Besides serving a gentleman." She winks at Christopher, and he blushes. "Have you seen Amelia?" She looks at me, turning to the side and motioning with her hand on her stomach. "Her feet have swelled up as big as watermelons. So, I did what any good cousin would do," she says. "I'm going to work the bar."

"You?" I ask. "Work the bar?"

"A lot has changed in six years," she tells me. "I may live at home, but I do work."

She walks to the end of the bar, and I pick up my beer and hold it out to Christopher. "To old times."

"Fuck, I hope not," he says, laughing while he clinks his bottle to mine, then brings it to his lips. "God, we were sad."

"We weren't that sad," I say, putting the bottle back on the bar.

"We were horny and sad," he says. "Two things that don't go together."

I laugh. "We went on dates." He nods now and looks over at Harlow. "You were dating Jenny when I left."

"Yeah," he says. "Best thing she could give me was my daughter and a divorce." I put my hand to my mouth.

"You married her?" I ask, shocked.

"She was having my kid," he says. "What was I supposed to do?" I look at him. He's got a point.

"Hey, do you remember Hazel?" I bring up her name, and he looks over at me, smirking.

"Hazel, who you chased for two months?" he asks, pushing my shoulder. "God, I thought for sure one day she would catch you with a boner. I used to follow you around waiting."

"Fuck you." I shake my head and bring the beer to my mouth. "She has a kid."

His eyes go wide. "No kidding."

"I guess she didn't hook up with anyone when I left?" I ask, and he shakes his head.

"No, we worked side by side for two months before we both left, and she said maybe five words to me," he says. "How old is her daughter?"

"No idea," I say, turning the beer bottle in front of me. I don't add that I'm going to find out.

Twelve

HAZEL

"I WANT TO see you at all times," I tell Sofia as she walks away from the front porch.

"Okay, Momma," she says, and I look over at her. She has always loved to go to the park, but seeing her here in my element is refreshing. Every day, she wants to put her overalls on and her Rubber boots. She doesn't care that her hands get dirty or that there is nothing to do but run freely. "Are you going to make it pretty today?"

"That's the plan." I look over at the weeds in the flower bed, and I want to tell her no. I've been trying to work on this fucking flower bed for the past five days. The first day, I walked into the barn with a pot and a spoon, holding my breath with Sofia behind me, and didn't find one fucking tool. The next day, I attempted to go into the "tool shed," and the door fell off in my hand, which made Sofia laugh like crazy. But also found no fucking tools. On the third day, I just gave up and decided that maybe it wasn't meant to be. Except I had this guilt the whole time, and yesterday, I finally gave up and went to buy what I needed. Six hundred dollars later, I now have tools to fix the flower bed and a lawn mower.

The sound of rocks crunching in the driveway makes me look up with a little bit of fear. It's been five days since Reed's visit, and I need to get out of here before more questions arise, and Reed puts two and two together. Casey came to see me the day after and said they were interested in buying the farm. I thought it would be the end of it, but he needed to make sure the house had no other liens. I thought it was going to be a one-day thing. I forgot that the South has their own time. Luckily for me, I still have vacation time from work, so I took an additional two weeks, but I need to get out of here. I'm testing fate by staying here. The white truck stops right behind my truck, and Sofia comes skipping over. "It's the horse man," she says, pointing at Billy as he gets out of the truck.

"I've been called worse," he says, laughing and waiting at the front of his truck while Charlotte gets out of the passenger side. I'm surprised to see them here since it's Sunday, and they usually, or at least they did, have their Sunday barbecue. It was something the town looked forward to. Even I used to enjoy them when we went. "How are you doing?" He looks over at me and then Sofia.

"Momma is making the flower bed pretty," she says, coming over to him. "She said bad words."

"Sofia." I call her name while Charlotte and Billy laugh. "It's been a challenge." I look over at the flower bed and then back at them. "I may have sworn a couple of times," I tell them so they can know without knowing that I'm taking good care of her. "But …" I shrug.

"What are you doing?" Charlotte asks while Sofia comes over and stands with them. Her hip is cocked to the side as she watches me.

"I thought I would clean up the flower bed," I start to say, lifting the shears that I have in my hand.

"Those look new," Billy says, and I nod. "Did you buy those?"

"Yeah, I couldn't find Pops' tools," I say sadly. "I looked everywhere."

"The door fell on Mom's head," Sofia interjects, and I glare at her. "She said a big bad word over and over again."

"Well, that settles it, then," Charlotte says, looking at Sofia, and I take a step down, thinking she is going to take her away from me. That they found out the truth and will take her from me. "How would you like to come to a barbecue?" she asks Sofia, who jumps up and down.

"And go on a horse." She gasps out as if you just told her that Santa Claus was coming, she looks over at me now.

"Momma, horses," she says, and my heart goes to my throat. "Can we go?"

"We aren't taking no for an answer," Charlotte says.

"So if you aren't there, I'm sending Billy back to get you," she tells me, and I know she isn't playing.

"I don't know. It's a family thing," I try to tell them. "We could maybe come tomorrow," I say, without adding *when no one else is there.*

"Nonsense," she says. "You are family." Little did she know just how close to the truth she was, at least for one of us.

"I can stay if you like," Billy says. "Take care of the flower bed while you get ready."

"No," I almost shout out. "Absolutely not. After what you did already for Sofia and me by buying this house," I say, blinking away tears. "Please just let me."

He nods his head at me and then looks at Charlotte. "We should go." Then he looks at Sofia. "See you soon, sunshine."

"Sofia." She thinks he forgot her name.

He laughs, squatting down in front of her. "But every time I see you, you are like a ray of sunshine." He taps her nose and then gets up. "Noon," he says, turning and holding Charlotte's hand as he walks her to the truck.

"I'm a sunshine," Sofia says, and I look back at her. *This is it,* I think to myself. I have two choices. I can pack up and leave or go to the barbecue and pray that Reed doesn't put two and two together. "Let's go, Momma," Sofia says, walking up the steps to the door. "We've got to take a bath." The decision is already made.

"We have to make something to bring to the barbecue," I say while she is in the bath. "You never go to someone's house without bringing food," I say. "It's a no-no."

She gets out, and I worry about what to dress her in. My stomach is a mess. My heart is beating so irrationally I hope I'm not having a heart attack. She picks out her pink shorts with a white T-shirt and gray sweater. I slip on my blue jeans and a white and blue button-down linen shirt. We both decide to leave our hair down.

I run downstairs while she plays on her iPad. Grabbing a straw basket, I put a checkered white and red dish towel on the bottom and fill it with the fresh loaves of bread I made today. I look over and see that it's already past noon. We walk out of the house after a little bit of an argument over her green Rubber boots. In the end, I didn't have the energy to fight with her.

The whole drive there, I think of maybe warning her, telling her not to talk to anyone. I play the scenarios in my head over and over again. The best thing is he doesn't figure it out; the worst is he gets it. I park on the street and get Sofia out. "We remember our manners," I say, grabbing the straw basket, and she just nods her head. I stop walking when I see Amelia waddling right in front of me. She turns and sees me, and her whole face lights up. "Oh my goodness," I say when we get close enough, and she gives me a big hug. Amelia was the one who gave me my first ever job and made sure I got all the shifts I needed during the summer to save up for school.

"Hazel," she says, smiling. "And who is this beautiful girl?" She looks over at Sofia.

"This is my daughter, Sofia," I say, and Sofia smiles at her.

"I heard you were back in town, and I was hoping I

would get to see you," Amelia says. "I'm sorry about Pops," she says sadly, and I nod. We turn to walk to the house where Asher is waiting for her. Asher smiles over at her and says something to her, but I don't know what else is said because the sound of my pounding heart is so loud in my ears.

Walking in with them is a little bit better than walking in on my own. Charlotte sees me and claps her hands, making all the women she is sitting with look over. My heart stops when I see Reed's mother, Olivia. She is and always will be the most beautiful woman I've ever seen. She gets up with Charlotte and Savannah, and they walk to me. "You came," she says, and I smile at her.

"I didn't think I had a choice," I answer her honestly.

"Momma made her special bread," Sofia says, putting her hand on the basket. "It's hot."

"Aren't you the cutest thing ever," Olivia says, rubbing her hand on her head, and just that touch makes the lump in my throat even bigger than before and tears sting in my eyes. "I heard that someone is waiting for you, and he has a horse."

"The horse man," she says, making everyone laugh again, but all I can do is look at her surrounded by her family.

"Do you mind if I take her to see Billy?" Charlotte asks, and I don't have time to say anything because Sofia walks over to her and grabs her hand.

"I guess that answers that," Olivia says, and she walks with Charlotte over to the barn.

"She'll be fine," Savannah says to me. "It can be

overwhelming." I smile at her.

"Where can I put the bread?" I ask, and she motions with her head to follow her. I take one look back over at Sofia and see that she is talking up a storm.

We walk over to the table, and I place the bread on it and open the towel that was on top of it. "Oh my goodness, what kind of bread is this?" Savannah asks.

"It's cranberry orange and white chocolate," I say, and she grabs a piece.

Her eyes go so big I think they are going to come out of her head. "This is …" She takes another bite. "The best thing I've had in my life." She grabs another piece.

"Are you a pastry chef?" she asks, and I laugh.

"I'm a CPA," I say. "Baking is my side stress reliever."

"Well, if you ever give up numbers," she says, grabbing another piece. "I suggest baking."

I laugh now. "I used to do it in college," I say, "after Sofia was born to make extra income." I shrug. "Now it's just for fun."

"Well, if you ever want to be really crazy, you can bake me a dozen of these before you go, and I'll buy them from you."

"That's not even the best one," I say. "My blueberry lemon scones." I point at her. "Now those."

"When do you think you'll be making those?" she asks, and I shrug.

"Hopefully, everything is cleared up this week, and I can get back to real life," I say. "But I'll make you some tomorrow."

She holds up her hand. "Pinky promise." I shake my

head and pinky promise with her. Kallie, Reed's aunt, comes over, and we catch up for a bit. By the time I look at my watch, two hours have already passed.

"I'm going to go and check on Sofia," I tell them, and they smile at me. I turn, walking back into the yard. There are kids everywhere. I look over to the side and see Hazel being chased by a boy her age and laughing the whole time. They run over to the fenced area, and she follows him in getting up on the bottom part to look over.

I'm making my way over to her when I see him walking from the other side of the property. He smiles and waves at a couple of people. "Maybe he won't see her," I say softly to myself. Even though I'm moving, I can't seem to get to her fast enough. It's almost as if my feet are stuck to the grass.

He stops when the little boy next to her calls him over, and I know it's only a matter of time before the box I closed all those years ago is opened.

Thirteen

Reed

I CAN HEAR the kids screaming as soon as I walk out of the woods and get closer and closer to my grandparents. I'm shocked so many people are still there. I thought for sure it would be dying down, but instead, it's like more people have arrived. I see Gabriel on the side as he chases another kid. I spot Amelia sitting down in a chair, her stomach even bigger than it was last week. I see a couple of teenagers off to the side, and it brings me back to all those years ago with Christopher. I smirk. Back then, I thought I was the shit.

I shake my head, stopping at the barn, and look around to see if I can find my grandfather. "Where were you?" Harlow says, walking out of the barn and looking at me. She has JB on her hip. "Go see Uncle Reed," she says.

He refuses to come to me by hiding his hand under him, making it hard to grab him, and Harlow laughs. "It's okay. He'll get to know you. He's used to you being in a phone." She laughs at her joke. "Quinn got here an hour ago."

"Did he?" I ask. "I actually went home and showered."

"I think he smells like shit all the time," she says, looking at JB and rubbing her nose to his. "See you later. I'm going to hand this boy off to someone else. I need some sleep," she says, walking away from me.

I stand here looking around, my gaze roaming everywhere, knowing exactly who I'm searching for. I look toward the house, and I see her standing there laughing with Amelia and Chelsea. Hazel, the whole reason I'm here two hours later than I should have been, stands looking toward the fence.

"Uncle Reed." I hear my name being called and look over to see Tucker. "Uncle Reed." He holds the top of the fence with one hand while he waves with his other. He is standing on the bottom of the log, looking into the fenced area. Some of the horses are walking around. He looks over to a little girl beside him and tells her something. One look at her, and I know she's Hazel's girl. She looks at him as if he's telling her his biggest secret. She wears green Rubber boots, and her brown hair has little curls at the bottom.

I walk over to them, and they both get down from the log. "That's my uncle Reed," Tucker says, pointing over at me.

"Hey," I say, looking at them both but my eyes are

on Sofia's. "What are you two up to?" I look at Tucker, and then my eyes go back to look at Sofia. She pushes the hair away from her face, and I see that her eyes are exactly like Hazel's.

"Sofia wants to ride the horse again," Tucker says. "But she said she doesn't have one."

"Well," I say, squatting down in front of her. "I have a horse." Her mouth opens, and her eyes go big. "Want to come ride on my horse?"

"Yes." She claps her hands together and jumps up and down. I swear it's like looking into a mirror, and I'm seeing Hazel from when she was young.

"Come with me," I say. She slips her hand into mine, and I can swear something in me sparks to life. "You coming, Tucker?" I ask, and he shakes his head.

"I'm going to eat," he says, turning now and running to the table where there is food.

We walk into the barn, and I go to my stall. "Is this your horse?" she looks up at me and asks.

"Yeah, my granddad gave it to me," I say. "Stay here," I say, opening the gate. Turning, I see her standing there with her hands on her hips and her head cocked to one side. I laugh, thinking I've seen that look before. I grab the horse by the reins and walk him out, going over to get my saddle. "We have to get the saddle on him," I say.

"So you don't hurt her?" she asks softly. "I don't want to hurt her."

I walk over to her and squat down. "It doesn't hurt her, sweetheart. I'm going to put you on the horse and then get on behind you."

I pick her up, and she opens her legs, sitting on the horse. "Hold on right here," I say, and she nods her head, grabbing the rein in her little hand.

I walk with the horse outside and see that Quinn is there with his daughter. "See them." I point at Quinn. "I'm going to get on like him."

"Okay," she says. I put my foot in the stirrup and sit on the horse behind her. She leans forward to whisper in the horse's ear. "It's okay." I put my arms around her, holding her in. She leans into my chest, and I smell the strawberry in her shampoo.

I move the horse toward Quinn. "Want to go to the trail?" I ask, and he nods his head. I look over at Hazel and see her standing there looking at us.

I motion with my head, and she just nods but doesn't say anything. Her eyes are on both of us. "So what's your name?" I ask as we follow Quinn as we go through the little trail that Ethan made when he had Gabriel.

"Sofia," she says proudly. "Sofia Bernadette."

"That's the perfect name," I say. "I used to be friends with your mom."

"You work at the office, too?" she asks, and I laugh, shaking my head.

"No," I say to her. "When she was little," I say.

"Did you know Pops?" she asks, looking up at me.

"Yeah, he was the best," I say.

"He had a tractor," she tells me. "It doesn't work."

"Did you ever ride on the tractor?" I ask, and she shakes her head.

"No, because it's broken," she tells me matter-offactly. "And now Momma said it's ready for the junkyard. I have a picture in my bedroom at my house."

"Do you?" I ask, and she nods.

"It's in my room. Not the one here." Her voice has to be the sweetest voice I've ever heard. "Now I sleep in Mommy's bed."

"I used to throw rocks at her window," I say, and she looks up at me. "Not big rocks. Ones just so she could come and talk to me."

"Why didn't you use the phone?" she asks, and I laugh.

"I don't know." She looks ahead. "You want to go fast?" I ask. Her eyes light up, and she tries not to smile, making me laugh. She is very much her mother's daughter, and I wonder if she knows her father, my chest getting a little twinge. "Okay," I say, putting an arm around her stomach and holding the reins in my free hand. I get the horse to trot just a touch faster, causing her hair to fly everywhere.

But the sound of her laughter is everything, and she holds on as tight as she can. "Faster, Uncle Reed," she says, and I laugh because she is copying Tucker. We finally get back to the barn, and she looks up. "That was so much fun," she says, looking over at Tucker who stands in the barn with Mayson.

"I'm going to get down first," I say, and she nods while I get down. I look up, holding out my arm, and she reaches for me, and I put her down.

"Thank you, Uncle Reed," she says, and Tucker comes over.

"It was my pleasure," I say, and she looks at Tucker.

"Did you see me?" she asks. "He went fast."

"My dad can go fast also," Tucker says, and I shake my head. I look over as I take off the saddle from the horse.

"Not as fast as Reed," she says, and he turns, running back to Mayson to ask him if he is faster than me.

I look over at Sofia, who stands there with her hip cocked. "Sofia," I call her name, and she looks over at me. I can't even try not to laugh at her. "Today was fun."

She nods her head at me. "I'm going to see my mom." She starts to run, then stops and turns back. "Thank you, Reed," she says, and when I smile at her, she smirks back at me. My whole body goes stiff, and everything in me screams. I'm about to take a step toward her when my grandfather comes to me.

"Hey," he says, and I look over at him and then look back over to see Hazel taking Sofia in her arms. "Did you finish?"

"Um, yeah," I say, my head spinning at this point. Did I just imagine it?

"Did you do both?" he asks, and I turn back and look at him with a confused look on my face. "Did you do the flower bed in the front and the back?"

"Yeah," I tell him. Before coming to the barbecue, my grandfather called and summoned me to his house. I thought I was coming to help set up for the barbecue. What I wasn't prepared for was my father and Quinn waiting for me. I got in the truck without asking questions, but as soon as we pulled up to Hazel's, I was informed we needed to fix the flower bed. "Nothing left in the front."

"Did you do the back also?" he asks, and my eyes roam the backyard again, hoping to see Hazel there, but I don't.

"We did around the deck," I tell him. "But that deck in the back is rotten. I'm surprised no one has gone through it."

"Shit," he says. "That's what I thought when I saw it." He nods at me and turns to walk away.

"Hey, Grandpa." I stop him, and he looks over at me. "What's the story with Sofia?"

"What do you mean?" he asks.

"How old is she?" I ask, and he shrugs.

"Why wouldn't her father be here?" I ask. "If his daughter is here, why isn't he?"

I stand here, and he crosses his arms over his chest, looking at me. "I don't know, Reed," he answers me. "What I do know is that little girl is a spitfire. Got on the horse for the first time today, and I swear to God. She looked over at me, she tucked in tight, and she was ready to go race him. She's got country in her." He smiles proudly. "Pops would be proud," he says, turning to walk back to the house.

I walk out of the barn, seeing my mother there. "Hey, Mom," I say. "Is Hazel around?"

"Um, I think she left." She looks around. "Have you met Sofia?"

"Yeah," I say, looking around.

"She called me Mrs. Princess," my mother says, putting her hand around my waist. I look down at her and

put my hand around her. "It's so good having you home."
I don't say anything to her because right now, my mind is at a house five minutes from here.

Fourteen

Hazel

I WALK OUT of the yard as fast as I can without it looking like I'm fleeing a crime scene. I smile at people as we walk out with Sofia's hand in mine. "Come on," I say to her, helping her get into the truck. I am not going to lie; the whole time, I thought Reed was going to come running and stop me. The fear that he makes a scene is too much to think about. I buckle her in and get into the truck and drive away. My eyes go to the rearview mirror to see if Reed is chasing the car.

I'm so nervous I'm shaking, and when I pull up in the driveway, I stop and look at the flower bed. "What in the dickens?" I say, seeing that all the weeds are gone. I put the truck in park, my eyes just looking at where the five-foot weeds were before we left. "Who?" I say, getting out of the truck and looking at it again to make sure my eyes are not playing tricks on me. Sofia knocks on the back window, and I walk over and open the door for her.

"You forgot me," she huffs out, and I just shake my head.

"Never," I say, and she walks ahead of me and stops.

"You did it, Mom," she says. "You cleaned all the fucking weeds."

"Don't say that." I point at her. "That is a bad word."

"I'm hungry," she says, walking up the front steps. I follow her and look over to see that fresh earth was put down also along with mulch. "Can you make me an egg to dig?"

She can never remember over easy. "Yeah," I say, ignoring all the questions spinning around in my head. "Go wash your hands," I say when I walk into the house and close the door behind me. She kicks off her rubber boots and leaves them at the front door. "You need a bath," I say, seeing her legs are dusty. "Let's get you a quick shower, and I'll make food after."

She walks up the stairs and undresses while I start the shower. She gets in, and I walk into the bedroom and sit on the bed for a second. My legs are still shaky from today. "It was not a good idea," I tell myself. "You're playing with fire." But seeing her with her cousins and with Billy, it was everything. The tears come now. When I was younger, it was my dream to be a part of a big family. It was everything I wished for. Now don't get me wrong, I loved my family. I loved that it was just Pops and me. But on Sundays, when we would go, I would wonder what it would be like.

"Momma." I hear her yelling. "I'm clean."

I wipe the tears away and walk back into the bathroom and dry her off. "There you go," I say, and she puts on her clothes. "Now, let's go eat."

She nods at me and walks down in front of me. She walks over to the kitchen table, grabbing her coloring book and coloring while I make her something to eat.

"Momma, did you ride horses?" she asks, and I look over at her.

"I did," I say. "Pops got me a horse when I was ten," I say. "We called him Ricky."

"I liked riding the horse," she tells me while she colors. "And I like Miss Charlotte and Mr. Billy."

"Me, too," I say, smiling at her and putting the egg and toast down in front of her.

"I liked Tucker," she says. "He was fun, and he said he was faster than me." She dips her bread into the egg. "We beat him on horses, too."

"Did you?" I sit down and watch her, my beautiful baby girl.

"Yeah, Uncle Reed is nice, too." I swallow the lump. "He said I could go back and ride the horse with him." She looks at me. "Can I, Momma?"

"We'll see," I say, my head screaming no.

"It was so much fun," she says, her eyes lighting up. "So many people." I don't say anything as she goes on and on about it between bites. When she is done eating, she asks to go lie down. "All the fresh air," she says, "kicked my butt." She rubs her eyes and slides into bed.

"Did you have fun today?" I ask as she lies down.

"I went on a horse two times," she says excitedly. "One with Billy and the other time with Uncle Reed." The minute she says that, I want to throw up. The heat rushes up my neck as I listen to her say his name.

"Uncle Reed," I say his name without wanting to.

"He said he used to throw rocks at your window," she tells me, and the tears come, but I wipe them away before she sees them.

"He did," I say, smiling. "It was a special code." She looks at me and closes her eyes. "Good night, sweet girl," I say, lying down with her. I hold her to me as my tears fall on my pillow.

When I looked around the barbecue and didn't see Reed, I sort of felt a sigh of relief. If he wasn't going to be there, I knew that I escaped the big one. I even let my guard down and sat down to talk to a couple of people.

My eyes were on Sofia the whole time. Her smile never left her face, and the sound of her laughter filled my ears. Then I saw him walking out of the forest. My heart started to speed up, and it was almost like I was having an out-of-body experience when he stopped beside her.

My heart sped up, knowing he was seeing her for the first time, and then it filled in my chest, knowing she just met her father. He smiled at her, and I got up. My first thought was to go and grab her and leave. But then she slipped her hand in his, and all I could do was watch. Watch my little girl get everything I wish I had.

He got on the horse with her and looked over at me. I just nodded as if to tell him she's yours. She looked over at me, and they both smiled, and it didn't take a DNA test to tell me what I already knew. He rode off with her, and I ducked out and went to the bathroom, where I let the tears come without fighting them off.

I made up excuses about having allergies when I walked out. My eyes roamed the field for them and I saw him with his hand around her waist to make sure she wouldn't fall off. The laugh coming out of her was everything. I always imagined they would meet one day. I always imagined that the minute he met her, he would know. He would feel it in his heart, and it would be so fucking amazing for both of them.

I close my eyes, and all I can see is them together. His smile and her smile—it's the same. I get up and walk back down the stairs to clean up the kitchen.

The soft knock on the door has me looking up. I knew it was coming. Even if I didn't want to admit it, I knew this day would come. The knock comes again, and this time, it's a bit louder than the last time. I unlock the door and open it, seeing him standing there. "Yes," I say, stepping out as he stands exactly where he did last week.

"I was wondering if you had a couple of minutes for me," he says, and I look at him, his eyes on mine. I don't answer him because I don't really think it's so much of a question.

"I met Sofia today," he says, looking up at me the whole time. For once, I'm happy it's dark outside, and I can't see his eyes, nor can he see the fear in mine.

"I saw." I cross my hands over my chest so he doesn't see them shaking. My mouth is suddenly dry as I try to swallow.

"She's," he says, and he puts his foot on the last step. He leans in, putting his hand on the railing. I watch him as he thinks about how to ask the question I know is coming. "She's something, a little bit of a firecracker," he says with a chuckle. "She does have one heck of a smile," he says, and my heart stops in my chest. "And a smirk I think I've seen before." I don't say anything, well, for one, I can't, even if I wanted to. "Let me ask you." His foot on the step is starting to shake now. "How old is she?"

I swallow down the tremors. "Five." I don't think I can say anything more without my voice cracking. I put my hands down to my sides. Looking at Reed, I see all of this going through his head.

"When is her birthday?" he asks, and I just look at him.

"March the first," I say, and he just stares at me.

"Is she mine?" he asks the loaded question. He asks the question that will change all of our lives. "Am I her father?"

I put my hand to my stomach. "If you are asking me if you share the same DNA," I say. "The answer is yes." His mouth now opens. "But if you are asking me if you are her father, the answer is no," I spit out, anger now coming through me, and apparently, I'm not the only one with anger in me.

"How could you?" he hisses out at me.

"How could I?" I ask, shocked, taking a step down now. "How could I? You made your stance pretty well-known when you couldn't so much as answer a fucking message," I say with hurt in my voice, but I don't even care anymore. I don't care because just like six years ago, the hurt is still there. The pain that I meant nothing to him destroyed me, but I put it away, blocked it out, but now, here in front of me, I can't deny it. The tears come one after another. "How you read the message and then just fucking deleted me." I don't stop. "Like I was nothing."

"It wasn't like that," he says.

"You can spin it whatever way you want to spin it, Reed," I say. "Bottom line, I reached out to tell you I was pregnant with our child. To tell you that I was going to keep our child and"—I shake my head—"you. Did. Nothing." I swallow now. "You read my message," I say. "I saw that you read it, and I waited. I waited all night for you to answer me, and you know what I got?" I say. "Sitting alone in a room with our child growing inside me." I stand straight. "I got nothing." I shake my head. "So you made your position known all those years ago." I shake my head and turn to walk up the stairs. "This talk is over."

"That is where you are wrong, Hazel," he says, and I can hear his voice is shaking. "This is just the beginning." I close my eyes as I walk into the house, and my legs give out.

Fifteen

Reed

THE SOUND OF the door closing has my heart breaking in my chest. The sound of her voice replays over and over. "If you are asking me if you share the same DNA, the answer is yes."

I sit on the step now, knowing that even if I tried to walk home, my legs would give out along the way. I hang my head. "A daughter." The tears come now as I remember her smile today. I missed it all because I was too busy trying to run.

The walk to my house is torture. The farther I get from them, the more my chest tightens. *"Bottom line, I reached out to tell you that I was pregnant with our child. To tell you that I was going to keep our child and ..."* I remember reading the message, remember how it fucked up my whole night. Remember yearning for home for the first time, and I also knew that if I gave in to it, I would be sucked back, and I'd be miserable my whole life.

Unlocking the front door of my house, I don't turn on a single light. Instead, I sit in the darkness as her words come back to kick me. *"Sitting alone in a room with our child growing inside me."* I want to know everything. I close my eyes, but nothing helps fight off the guilt. Not one thing I have done or said will make up for missing five years.

The sun comes up, and I know I have to talk to her. I know that things need to be said, so I walk back over to the house. Walking up the three steps, I knock softly. I didn't even check what time it is. I don't have time before the door opens just a bit. Her little eyes see me, and they light up. "Momma," she says over her shoulder, opening the door. "It's Uncle Reed." Hazel comes out of the kitchen with her hair tied up on top of her head, wearing shorts and a T-shirt. "Momma is making pancakes," she says.

"Go sit and eat," Hazel says to her, and I can't stop from looking at her. She stands there with her hip cocked just like I'm standing right now. Her smile is the most beautiful thing in the whole world.

"Later, Uncle Reed," she says, and I shake my head and try not to laugh.

I wait for her to be out of the room before looking at Hazel. The dark circles under her eyes show me that she didn't sleep either. "Hey," I say softly.

"Come in," she says, and I step in and close the door

behind me. "Um …" She starts to talk, and I hold up my hand.

"Before you say anything, I'm sorry, Hazel," I say. "There is no excuse for any of my actions."

"I wanted to tell you," she says, and I can finally see her eyes. The sadness in them, the tears. "But I …"

"I should have answered. That is on me," I say.

"We have a lot to talk about," she says, and I just nod my head.

"Will you promise me that you won't leave?" I ask her, my heart clenching in my chest as if someone is reaching in and squeezing it with all their might. "At least not before we talk things out."

"I don't know how long we will be here," she says. "But I promise that if we leave, I'll tell you beforehand."

I just nod at her. "I've got someplace to be," I say, and she just looks at me. I want to reach my hand up and hold her face. Right before I kiss her lips. "But if it's okay, I'd like to come back and see Sofia."

"That's fine," she says softly.

"Bye, Sofia," I say, holding my hand up, and she looks up from her plate.

"Bye, Uncle Reed," she says, and I look at Hazel, who has her eyes closed.

"She has never called anyone uncle before," she tells me. "I don't even know if she knows what that means."

"Tucker called me that, so she might think that's my name," I say, not telling her that by the end of all of this, she is going to be calling me dad.

"See you later," I tell them both and turn to walk out

of the house.

Taking my phone out of my pocket, I call my father first, and he answers right away. "Hey, son," he says.

"Hey, Dad," I say, looking around and seeing that the fucking property needs to be fixed. "I was wondering if you have a couple of minutes to sit down with me."

"This sounds serious," he says, and I look back at the door.

"It is," I say. "Where are you?"

"Headed out to the clubhouse now," he says.

"I'll see you there," I say, hanging up the phone and running home. I get into the truck and make my way over.

The only car in the parking lot is my father's. I get out and walk into the converted barn. The white door closes, and once I walk in, I hear a buzzing noise. I pull the door open and step inside my father's world. From the looks of it, he looks just like a regular cowboy, but he's so much more. He's one of the best computer tech people I know with a massive contract to the military as well as the security measures around the world.

He sits at a desk, leaning back in it with a coffee in his hand. "Now I know it's serious," he says to me, and I shake my head. "Also, you look like shit."

"Wow," I say, putting my hand to my chest. "That hurt." He just shrugs.

"I'm not going to piss on your leg and tell you that it's raining. You look like trash. Have you slept?" he asks, putting down his cup of coffee, and I look at him. My stomach clenches when I think of telling him about Sofia.

"I've had things on my mind," I say, sitting down and wondering how disappointed he's going to be in me for not taking responsibility for my child. "I've been thinking." My leg is starting to shake when I start talking. "What would you say if I asked you for a job?" I look over at him, and his eyebrows pinch together.

"I would say why?" His eyes look into mine, and I wonder if he can tell how desperate I am.

"I don't understand." I laugh nervously. "Do you not want me to work for you?"

"Oh, no, you don't," he says, shaking his head and grabbing his mug again. "You aren't turning this around on me." He puts his mug down. "You were dying to get out of this town. Dying," he says the word again. "And now, all of a sudden, you want to work here." He shakes his head. "That doesn't jibe." He puts his hands together. "Now let's start this again. Why do you want to work for me?"

"I can't tell you right now," I say honestly.

"You can tell me anything, you know that, right?" my father says, the worry all over his face. "If you need money or you're in trouble."

I shake my head. "I'm not in trouble, Dad." I feel like throwing up. "Nor do I need money." I shrug. "I just." I think about the right words to say. I think about how to word it, and the only thing that comes to my mind is what I say next. "I found my purpose," I tell him the truth. She is five years old, and she is the best thing I've ever done.

"Then I say"—he swallows, and tears form in his

eyes—"you've got a job whenever and wherever you want it."

"I don't want you to just say that or to just give me a job to give me money," I say. "If I stay and do this, I want to earn the money just like everyone else."

"No one is going to give you anything, son," he tells me. "If you want it, you have to earn it."

"I can work with that," I say and get up. "I'll get back to you."

"The offer is there whenever you want," he says, and then I look down and take one step away. "I don't know what you are hiding …" I stop in my tracks, looking over at him. "But whatever it is." He swallows now. "It brought life back into your eyes." I smirk at him, not sure I can say another word without pouring out my heart to him. Without sitting with him and telling him about Sofia. About missing everything because I was a selfish bastard. About how she smiles like me and how she has the same smirk as both of us. About how fucking amazing she is, and I've only spent an hour with her.

"See you later," I say, turning and walking out of the clubhouse. I get into the truck, knowing who else I need to talk to.

When I get to the gym, I walk in and find Ethan on the treadmill running. "Now you show up," he says to me, not breaking his stride or huffing out. "A little late, don't you think?"

"Yeah," I say to him and then walk to the machine where he continues to run. "I had something to do." He just looks over at me, and I stand here with my hands in my back pockets. "What would you do if you were still enlisted in the service?"

"What do you mean?" he asks and lowers the speed of the treadmill.

I think about how to word the question without making him suspect anything. "If you were in the service and you had Gabriel and Audrey back home, would you think about leaving?"

"If I still had time on my contract, then I would have no choice," he says. "But if I wasn't enlisted, I wouldn't be able to leave them."

"Lots of guys do it." I point out to him. "I had seven brothers who all had families back home."

"And I have so much respect for them. Not only are they serving the country and keeping us safe." He shuts down the treadmill. "I don't know how they do it." Grabbing his water bottle, he takes a large pull. "To be away from your wife and kids all the time for months on end." He shakes his head. "It must be fucking torture."

"I mean, you get to come home on leave." I wait for him to answer me.

"Yeah, and you get to watch your kids grow up via a fucking phone." He takes another pull of water. "Again, I have respect for them, but if something happened to either of them when I was away, I would not be able to forgive myself or look at myself in the mirror. Waking up every single day to my son and my daughter. You can't replace that. Not for all the money in the world."

My stomach sinks when he puts it like that. I knew last night when I sat on my couch what I needed to do. I knew in my heart that it would lead to this conversation. I knew that in the end I would think exactly how Ethan thinks. I knew, in the end, I would not leave her. “Thanks,” I say, and he just nods at me.

“Is there something you aren’t saying?” he asks, and I just shake my head. In time, I will tell him the truth, but for right now, it’s going to be my secret.

Sixteen

HAZEL

"MOMMA," SOFIA CALLS my name from the kitchen. "I'm finished." I grab the tray of blueberry scones out of the oven and put them on the stovetop. I've been baking all morning long to keep my mind off Reed. Him showing up here this morning shocked me. To be honest, I thought it was either Billy or Casey, which is why I told Sofia to get the door.

Seeing him stand there with his eyes just as red as mine. Both of us looked like we didn't sleep all night, and I can say I didn't. I thought about packing it all up yesterday and leaving. I ran it over in my head, but then I looked over at Sofia and knew that she deserved better. She deserves for me to give him a chance and hear him out. For her. She deserves it all. So much so I called work and asked them for a month off. My stomach was in my throat the whole time, and I wondered if they would even give it to me, but I knew if they didn't, I would give them my resignation letter. I have a good-size savings, and I know I will be able to get a job.

"Be right there," I say, taking off my oven mitt and walking over to her. I sit down next to her and grab the papers she was working on. "Let's see what you did here." I smile at her and look at the worksheet she's working on. "You did good."

"Can we go play outside now?" she asks, and I look over at the stove clock.

"Let me just clean up a bit," I say. "Why don't you go and grab a couple of books and read them to me?" I say, and she gets off the chair and runs to the living room, coming back with four books. "Which one are you going to read first?" I ask, wetting a rag and turning to wipe down the counters that are splattered with flour. Something I should have known when I gave Sofia the electric whisk and a bowl of flour. The knock on the door has me stopping, and I look over at Sofia. My stomach sinks and my heart speeds up when I hear the knock again.

I put the rag down, walking over to the door, bracing myself for what is to come. I pull it open, and my eyes widen when I see Savannah standing there. "Hey." She smiles at me and puts her sunglasses on her head. "I'm sorry to just drop in. But I was hoping you had some time to talk to me."

"Oh my gosh," I say, shaking my head. "Please come

in." I move to the side, and she comes in. She smells like a garden. Her black hair is in a ponytail as she wears white jeans and a pink shirt. "Please come in," I say and then smile. "I just took my blueberry scones out of the oven."

She gasps out. "Well, if this isn't just my day." She follows me to the kitchen. "There she is," Savannah says, going over to Sofia and squatting down beside her. "I must have heard your name over a hundred times today." She taps her nose with her finger. "Were your ears ringing?"

Sofia puts her hands to her ears. "Momma, my ears ring," she says, making us both laugh, and I shake my head.

"No, honey," Savannah tells her. "Your ears ring when people are talking about you." She looks at Savannah, shaking her head.

"They didn't ring." She looks at me. "Did you hear it?"

"I think I did a bit," I say, and she just shrugs and turns back to her book.

"Can I get you something to drink?" I ask Savannah as she stands up. "I just made some sweet tea," I say, walking over to the fridge. "Not going to lie. I have not made that in a while." I take out the glass jug from the fridge.

"I'll take whatever you are having," Savannah says, getting up. I pour her a glass of sweet tea and one for myself also, grabbing a small plastic cup for Sofia. I grab the lemon icing and slowly pour some over five scones, placing them on a plate.

I place the plate in the middle and look at Sofia, who is already reaching out to grab one. "Don't you dare," I say, and she stops midway. "Let me get you a plate," I say, turning and walking to get small plates. "Okay, which one do you want?" She gets up, leaning over the table. "Pick one."

She sits there looking at all of them, and I look over and see Savannah with the biggest smile. "It's a hard choice," she tells her. "But I think they all look good."

"This one." She points at the one nearest to her. I place it on her plate and hand Savannah hers. "You can choose yours," I say, and she laughs.

I sit now with a plate and choose my own. "Oh my God," Savannah says with a full mouth. "Oh my God." I smile, proud that they turned out good. "These are …" she says, closing her eyes and just savoring them. I take my own bite, and the tang of the citrus hits my tongue right away, and then the sweetness from the fresh berries fills my mouth.

"It's good, Momma," Sofia says on her knees. "Can I watch television?" I get up, grabbing her plate and her cup, and carry it over to the living room. I put on her show, and she sits down on her little stool watching it.

"I'm having another one," Savannah says when I walk back to the kitchen.

"I made three dozen," I say, and her eyes get big, and she wiggles her eyebrows.

"How does it feel to be back?" she asks, chewing.

"It's different," I answer her, taking my own bite.

"But then again, it's like coming home. If that makes any sense."

"It totally does," she says. "Doesn't coming home feel good?" Grabbing a napkin and cleaning her hands. "It's why I came over, actually." I look at her, not saying anything, and I suddenly get hot around my neck, the sweet tea looking to come back up. "I don't know if you've been to town yet," she says.

"A couple of times," I say. "When I got to town and then when I went to see Mr. Devlyn."

"I don't know if you saw the new little strip mall that the town just put in." She takes a bite of her scone.

"The one next to the diner?" I ask, wondering if there is another one and then thinking I really need to go into town and see what else has changed.

"Yes," she says. "The town decided that it needed more commercial businesses in order to drum up tourists."

"That sounds like a great idea," I say. "What are they thinking of putting there?"

"So far we have a beauty salon and spa," she says. "A flower shop, and I was hoping that we could have a little coffee shop."

"Wouldn't that be too close to the diner?" I ask. "They sell coffee."

"Yes," she says, leaning in now. "But I want a little coffee shop where you can go in and grab a cookie and a latte or iced coffee."

"Yes," I say, nodding my head. "There is one like that right near where we live, and they have the best cheese danishes alive."

"Exactly." She points at me. "That is exactly what I was thinking. Some small tables, opens in the morning, and closes at five."

"I would go," I tell her, and she gets excited. "If I lived here, that is."

"Well, what would you say if I told you that I want to open the shop?" she says, and I tilt my head to the side. "And I want you to be my business partner." My eyebrows pinch together.

"I'm a CPA," I say. "Do you need help with the books?"

"Well …" She looks down, and I can sense she is nervous. "I was hoping you would help me run it and …" Her voice goes low. "That you would handle the baking side of the business."

I look at her shocked. "Again," I say. "I'm a CPA, not a baker."

"That bread you had was the best bread I've ever had, and it's not just me. Everyone who came and had it has called Charlotte, asking for her recipe." My mouth hangs open. "These scones would sell out in thirty minutes."

"I'm not here for much longer," I say. "I have a month, and then I have to be back at work. I just came to tie all the loose ends together."

"What if you didn't leave?" she says, and I just sit here. The thought never ever crossed my mind.

"I have a life," I say. "A full-time job. Friends. Sofia's school."

"You could have that here and be your own boss," she says and holds up her hand. "Don't tell me just yet. Why don't you think about it and let me know?"

"I just sold this house to Casey," I say. "I have a …" I don't continue talking because she leans over and puts her hand on mine.

"Maybe this was meant to be," she says, looking at me, her blue eyes crystal. "Maybe you were meant to come home and stay." Thoughts in my head spin around and around as I think of her words. "You don't have to make a decision right now. Why don't you meet me in a couple of days and we can look over things?" she tells me. "Then you can decide."

She pushes the chair away from the table. "Let me pack up some scones." I get up and grab a Tupperware container and put a dozen in there, placing the lid on it but not closing it. "You have to let it have a little air, or they will get soggy," I say, and she grabs it from me and smells them.

"I might have to eat one in the car," she says, turning to say bye to Sofia.

"Thank you," she says when I walk her to the door and outside. "For the hospitality."

She gets in the car, and I watch her drive off. Sitting on the porch looking out at the driveway and then turning to see the flower bed, I wonder if it's meant to be. I can almost hear Pops' voice clear as day talking to me. "You never know until you try." The tears now come without me even knowing. "I really wish you were here, Pops," I say, my head hanging.

"No." I shake my head, getting up now. "It was not meant to be. None of this was meant to be," I say more to myself. “In a month, I will say goodbye to this town just like I did six years ago.” I walk back inside, and I can hear Pops laughing in the distance.

Seventeen

Reed

"YOU LOOK LIKE shit," Quinn says, coming into the barn in his workout clothes, looking at me as I get off the treadmill.

"Right back at you," I say, looking at his bloodshot eyes. "You are even walking hunched over."

"That's what happens when you fall asleep in a rocking chair." He closes his eyes. "I should just go and nap over there." He points at the mats in the corner. "No one would know." I laugh at him.

"Why the fuck would you fall asleep in a rocking chair?" I ask, taking a sip of water and smirk at him. "Is it because Willow kicked you out of bed?"

"No," he hisses. "It's because Grace is teething, and nothing would help her. Except rocking." He puts his head back and rubs his neck. "What's your excuse?"

"Just thinking," I say, not sure what to say just yet. Before announcing to everyone I have a daughter, I want to get to know her. "I'm going to head out. Take a nap," I say, walking out and then turning. "Besides, I heard dad bods are all the rage these days."

"Fuck you," he says, and I laugh, running back to the house and jumping in the shower. I slip on another pair of jeans and a T-shirt, grabbing the keys to the truck and walking out of the house.

After I spoke with Ethan, the decision was already cemented in my head. I made a list of things that I had to do, and the first step was going to the bank. Walking in, I nod at a couple of people. "How may I help you?" the blonde behind the desk asks when I step up.

"I called Clarence this morning," I say. "He was going to have an envelope ready for me." She turns and grabs a stack of envelopes. "It's for Reed Barnes." She looks through the white envelopes, finally finding mine.

"Here it is." She hands it to me, and I grab it, putting it in my back pocket. Walking out, I put my sunglasses on and head over to my grandfather's barn.

I park the truck in the driveway and walk over through the backyard, the same backyard I met my daughter in for the first time. The same backyard that I want my daughter to grow up running in, but I know that I am getting ahead of myself. I look back at the house to see if my grandmother is there, but I don't see her. I walk past the fence and into the barn seeing Asher there with my grandfather as they go over something. They both look up at me. “Boy, you look …” I hold up my hand.

“If one more person tells me I look like shit,” I say, shaking my head, and they both laugh.

“If the shoe fits,” my grandfather says. “You look like a man on a mission.”

“I kind of am,” I say and then look at Asher, who senses I need to speak to my grandfather alone.

“I have to get back home to Amelia,” he says. “She is going to the doctor for her forty-second-week checkup,” he says, and my grandfather chuckles. “Also, she hates me. But I’ve been told it’ll be good once she has the baby.”

I roll my lips. “She told me she’s castrating you as soon as she has the baby.” His face goes white.

“It’s not my fault that I make big babies.” He throws up his hands, turning and walking out.

“Poor son of a bitch,” my grandfather says, watching Asher get into the sheriff’s truck. “She is going to eat him alive.”

“I think he’ll be fine,” I say, then turn to look at my grandfather, who is just staring at me.

“What’s gotten into you?” he asks.

“I want to buy a horse,” I say, and he just looks at me.

“You have a horse,” he says. “She’s parked in stall three.”

“I want to buy another horse,” I say, and I know he’ll have questions.

“So pick a horse,” he says, and then I shake my head.

“I want to pay for it,” I say, and he throws his head back and laughs.

"You aren't paying for shit, son," he says. "If I take your money, you know what is going to happen?" I roll my eyes. "One, your grandmother is going to skin my hide alive." He holds up one finger and then another. "Two, your father is going to come over and rip up the check. And three, I'll just give it back to you when I die."

I put my head back. "Why do you always have to do the 'when I die' shit?" I say.

"If you don't want to hear it, don't come throwing your money at me," he says. "We just got seven new horses this morning. Quinn is going to have to take a couple to train for his therapy camp, but I think I have one in mind for you," he says, turning now and walking out of the barn, and I follow him. "Let's see if we think alike." The sound of horses running makes me look into the enclosed fence area. We walk up to the logged fence, and I stand next to my grandfather as we look at the horses. My eyes go to one horse in particular. "Go pick," my grandfather says, and I nod at him.

I take off my shirt and put it on the fence. "Is there a reason you are taking off your shirt?" Ethan says, coming in with Gabriel by his side. "You planning on buying her dinner, too?"

"Still jealous about my six-pack." I wink at him and turn to walk into the area. "You'll get yours back."

"I still have my six-pack!" he shouts at me. "It's just four at the moment."

"Whatever you have to tell yourself." I clap my hands and walk over to the caramel-colored horse. She looks up at me, and I see her beautiful brown eyes. The hair on the top of her head is white, and she has a white mark between her eyes. She looks at me up and down and takes a step back from me.

"I'm not going to hurt you." I put up my hand, and she takes a couple more steps away from me. "It's okay." Her tail goes right and left as she waits for me. "I'm not going to hurt you." She lets me touch her before moving away, her eyes on my hand the whole time. "No one is going to hurt you, girl," I say and take a step to her, rubbing her neck. "I have a little girl," I say, my chest filling up so much I feel like it's going to explode. "She's amazing, and she's beautiful. She's kind, and she loves horses." The horse puffs out now as if she understands me. "And I want her to have a horse that loves her as much as I do." I make my way to the other side of the horse, seeing if she is going to do anything. "Okay, let's take you for a ride," I say as I mount her.

She doesn't buck me off, so I'm already winning. "Attagirl," I say to her and make her trot. "There you go," I say.

"Why isn't he wearing a shirt?" I look over and see Emily with her hand over her eyes to block the sun while she looks at me.

"He thinks he's John Wayne," my grandfather says, and I laugh. I take her for a ride in the forest to see how she reacts to sounds, and she is perfect. A touch scared, but she'll do. I ride her back to the barn. Getting off and grabbing the reins, I bring her to the water. She walks with me slowly, and when we get close to the barn, she stops.

"I'm here," I say, and she takes one step and then another, stopping every four steps to look around to see where she is.

"Hey, John Wayne," my grandfather says, coming out of his office, laughing. "How did she do?"

"She did okay in the forest; the noises didn't spook her," I say, getting her in the stall and showing her the fresh water. "She'll be fine." I rub her neck. "I'll take her."

"Already put it down in the book," he says, and I laugh.

"What happened to the computer?" I ask, knowing full well how much he hates it. It's as old-school as it gets. It took four years for him to agree to the flip phone he still has.

"That thing got jammed." He shakes his head. "Now Harlow comes in the morning, takes all my papers, and does what she needs to do with them."

I laugh now and walk out of the barn. "Thanks, Grandpa," I say, walking to his desk and putting my shirt back on. "I'll come back later today." I think to myself, hoping I can convince Hazel to let me bring Sofia here. "Or tomorrow."

He looks at me. "This is your home," he says. "You never have to tell me when you are going to be here. You come when you want to come."

I didn't know how much I needed to hear that right now. "Thank you, Grandpa," I say. "For everything."

He nods, unsure what I'm talking about, and I know that I'm going to have to sit down with him and tell him.

After my parents, he is the one I want to tell the most. I walk away from him, heading to my truck and going to the one place I've been wanting to go back to since this morning.

I pull up in the road that leads to the house and park behind the truck. I get out now and look over through the tall grass and see her hopping by herself. I watch her, and I swear to God I can't explain it, but I would do anything in the world for her. She looks up now and sees me. "Uncle Reed!" she yells and runs to me, pushing her hair behind her ears. I squat down now as she gets close. "Did you think about me?" she asks, and I look at her smiling. "My ears were ringing." She laughs, and I want to take her and pull her to me and kiss her neck. I want to tell her how sorry I am for not being there for her first step. I want to tell her how sorry I am for missing everything.

"I thought about you all day," I say, blinking away the tears. "Where is your mom?" I ask, looking around.

"She is making me cookies 'cause I fell, and I bleeded." She points at her knee. "Over a fucking rock." I roll my lips.

"I don't think you should say that word," I say. "Where did you fall?"

"Over there." She points at the tall grass. "I didn't see it, and I fell."

I reach out and touch her knee with my finger. "I bet you were really brave," I say, and she shrugs. "What kind of cookie is Mom making?"

"Chocolate chip." She smiles now. "Is that your

favorite?"

"It is." I don't add in that it is now. "It's my favorite."

The door opens now. "Sofia!" Hazel yells her name, and her eyes find mine. "Come get cookies."

I look back to see Hazel standing on the porch. "Momma," Sofia says. "Uncle Reed was thinking about me all day. My ears were ringing." She starts walking, then turns and comes back to slip her hand in mine. "Come on, I'll share my cookies with you."

Eighteen

Hazel

I OPEN THE door and yell her name. "Sofia. Come get cookies." I look for her, and my eyes find Reed. My heart speeds up as I watch the two of them.

"Momma!" Sofia yells. "Uncle Reed was thinking about me all day. My ears were ringing." She starts to walk to me and stops, turning back and going back to Reed. She slips her hand in his and looks up at him. "Come on, I'll share my cookies with you."

The lump in my throat grows even bigger as they walk toward me. He's wearing jeans and a white shirt, and he's even hotter than he was six years ago. He made my stomach flutter even back then, but now that he's all grown up, he's taken it to a whole different level. "We have to wash our hands," she tells Reed. "Or no cookies."

She walks into the house, and Reed stops in front of me. "Hey," he says softly. "I didn't."

I just shake my head. "It's fine." He walks in, and I wait a couple of seconds before walking in. Putting my hand to my stomach, I let out the breath I was holding when he walked by me. This whole day has been one thing after another, starting with him showing up here this morning. Then Savannah came over, only to have Sofia fall and scratch her knee. The sound of her shrieking made my blood run cold. I got there in record time, and I was expecting to find something broken. The blood was running down her leg in thick drops. I carried her in and cleaned the area, thinking for sure she would need stitches. How the fuck would this look to Reed? I've second-guessed every single thing I've said and done since he found out that Sofia is his.

"You put soap." I hear Sofia. "And then you sing your ABCs," she sings now. "Now I know my ABCs, won't you come and play with me," she sings louder. "Now you can rinse." I walk into the kitchen and see her sitting on the counter, knowing he picked her up and put her there. "See," she says, turning now and grabbing the rag, and semi wiping her hands down. "All clean."

"Thank you," Reed says when she hands him the towel. He wipes his hands and now picks her up, and I see that he wants to kiss her cheek, but all he does is smile at her. His eyes are filled with all the love I thought they would be.

"Momma," Sofia says, looking at me. "Can we have a cookie before the spaghetti?" she asks, and I look over at Reed.

"I usually don't feed her dessert before dinner." I have this crazy need for him to know that I'm a good mom. "It's just, she fell before, and I ..."

He holds his hand up to stop me from talking, and I thank God since I have a feeling I would have word vomited. It's like I can't stop saying the wrong thing. "Sometimes, a cookie before dinner makes you even hungrier." He smirks at me. "But only one."

"Okay, one," Sofia says and then looks over at me, and she has the same smirk her father has. *I am such an idiot,* I think to myself. How could I think he wouldn't see it? How could I have thought that coming back here was a good idea?

"Come and sit, Uncle Reed," Sofia says. "I can read," she tells him, getting on her chair and sitting on her knees. "See this, it's *Green Eggs and* Ham." She holds up the orange book, and Reed sits down next to her. I walk over and put two cookies on a plate and then bring it over to them. "I get to pick first," Sofia says. "Because I'm smaller."

Reed laughs at her now. "Those are the rules," he says, smiling at her, and she picks up her cookie.

"This one is bigger." She takes a bite. "Yummy."

The timer on the stove dings, and I walk over and take the pasta off the stove, straining it in the colander, "Did you eat?" I ask, not looking at him.

"No. I'm sorry," he says. "I didn't even think about the time."

"Uncle Reed," Sofia says. "Did your ears ring today?"

she asks him, and I close my eyes as I listen to the next part. “I was thinking about you.” One tear comes out now and rolls down my cheek.

“Did you?” he says, and I can just imagine how that must feel for him.

“Yeah. And your horse,” she says, making him laugh.

“If your momma says it’s okay, maybe we can go for a ride tomorrow,” he says, and I hear her gasp out.

I turn and walk over to put the pasta in the saucepan, mixing it. “Momma.

“Can we?” she asks, and my eyes never leave the pan in front of me.

“We’ll see,” I say, grabbing a plastic plate for her. I turn to get a fork and knife to cut it.

“Can I help?” Reed pushes away from the table, and I can feel him beside me. “I can cut that for her.”

“Yeah, sure,” I say, not sure how I feel about him stepping up. This is what you wanted, my head screams. This is what you hoped for the whole time. I place some pasta on a plate and then fill Reed’s with more than mine. I carry them to the table, my hands shaking a bit. It’s a good thing I set the table for us before he got here. I walk back to grab another pair of utensils while he finishes cutting her pasta. He brings it to the table and places it in front of her.

“It’s still hot,” he tells her. “So you need to blow.” I sit down, facing Reed as he sits.

“Don’t eat,” Sofia says. “We have to say grace.” She turns her hand over for his and then the other one for me. I put my hand in hers, and Reed reaches across the table for mine. My hand slowly reaches across the table, his hand facing up. His hand is warm to my cold one. “Dear God,” Sofia starts, and I look over and see that her eyes are closed. My eyes go to Reed’s as he just stares at me. “Thank you for the cookies and the food,” she says. “And for Uncle Reed and his horse.” Reed chuckles while the emotions get the better of me. “Amen.”

“Amen,” I say before I get up. “Excuse me,” I say, rushing up the stairs and to the bathroom.

I close the door and put my hand to my mouth. The sob comes out as quiet as I can, my back against the door as I slide down to my ass. I wipe away the tears that come right after the other, and the soft knock on the door makes me stop.

“Hazel.” I hear his voice softly. “Are you okay?”

“Yeah. I’ll be right down,” I say, getting up now, listening to hear him walk away. I get up, making my way over to the sink and opening the water. Rinsing off my face, I grab the towel and dab the water off.

Opening the door, I’m not expecting him to be there waiting for me, leaning against the wall with his ankles crossed. “Oh,” I say out loud and stop in my tracks. “I thought.”

“What’s wrong?” he asks softly and looks down the stairs to make sure that Sofia isn’t coming up.

“Nothing,” I tell him, looking down. “I’m fine.”

“You aren’t fine,” he says. “It might have been six years ago”—he stops and swallows—“but I know you.”

“That was a long time ago,” I say, my knees feeling like they’re going to buckle when I look up at him and see his eyes. His eyes always felt like he could see into my soul, and that never went away. The same look he used to give me as we spent all those nights talking in the barn. I knew as time went on that I was slowly falling in love with him. I knew it was stupid and would only lead to me being heartbroken when he went away, yet I did it anyway.

"Not that long." He doesn't move, and I know that if I don't say anything, he isn't going to drop it.

"It's just," I start to say. My lip tremors, and he stands up now and comes closer to me. He stands right in front of me as I try not to cry. "It's just that for our whole life, it's just been her and me." I wipe the tear as fast as I can. "No matter what, it was always just us." He starts to say something, and I hold up my hand to stop him. "Every single day, it was us two at the table, except when Pops came to visit. So seeing you at the table with her and her thanking God for you." I close my eyes, taking slow, soft breaths. "It was just so real. I've thought about this moment for the last six years. I've thought about how you would be with her. And it's just so much better than I thought it was going to be." I fidget with my hands. "I've always wanted her to have what she had yesterday and today." His hand comes up now as his thumb stops a tear from rolling down my cheek. "You have no idea how it felt seeing her running, knowing that she was with family. Knowing that she had all these people there for her and that they didn't know."

"There are going to be more days," he says, his hand not moving from my face. "I don't want to take your place. I just want to have a place where I get to love her also."

"I'll never ever keep her from you," I say, and his thumb rubs my cheek. "Not now, not ever."

"There are things we need to talk about," he says, and I feel my stomach rise and fall. "There are things that need to be said, but I don't want to do it now when she is up or can hear."

"You're right," I say. "There are things that need to be said."

"Let's finish eating, and then I'm going to take off. I'll come back tonight, and we can talk." I nod my head, not sure I can answer him. "But just so you know, Hazel, I'm not going anywhere."

He doesn't say anything more. His hand drops from my face, and he walks back down the stairs. My hand comes up to my face where I can still feel his touch, his words echoing in my head. *"I'm not going anywhere."*

Nineteen

Reed

I WALK DOWN the stairs, my hand still tingling from touching her face. My thumb is still wet from her tears. I saw her get up from the table, saw the tears, and my heart broke. Thinking that my being here was hurting her, I couldn't breathe, couldn't move. I looked over at Sofia to see if she noticed, but all she did was eat her spaghetti.

I walk back down, sitting down in the chair right next to Sofia, and she just looks up at me with sauce all over her cheeks. "Is it good?" I ask, and she nods her head. I want to lean over and kiss her, but I don't know if it's too fast. I want to hold her in my arms all the time. Carry her to make up for all the years I didn't.

I hear the stairs creak and look up to see Hazel come back and sit down. Her beauty stops everything in me.

All the thoughts are gone, and the only thing I can think of is making this right here something that I do every night. She looks over at me, and she gives me a side smile and takes her first bite of pasta.

I take my time eating, knowing that as soon as I finish eating, I'm going to have to leave and my stomach sinks thinking about it. "So what grade are you in, Sofia?"

"Kindergarten," she answers, filling her spoon with pasta.

"Do you like school?" I take my own bite.

"Yeah, but sometimes it's boring," she says, moving her head. "And the math is too easy."

I laugh at her expression. "Do you like math?" I ask.

"She's doing math at a third-grade level," Hazel says. "She has always loved it. We started practicing her addition when she was three," she lets me know, and I smile at her.

"Definitely takes after her mom for that," I say, smirking and grabbing another bite. Hazel always did better in school than I did. If I got a sixty, I was happy with it.

"She goes to private school also," she tells me, and I just nod. "She's getting a good education."

"I don't doubt it," I say, sensing that she's nervous when it comes to talking about Sofia.

"I drop her off and pick her up as soon as she's done her extra-curricular activities." She pushes the pasta around her plate.

"What do you do extra?" I look at Sofia.

"Chess," she says, and my eyes open wide. "And

math club."

"Definitely a momma's girl," I say, laughing, and she smiles.

"I look like my momma," she says, and I just nod.

"You are just as beautiful as your momma," I say and look over at Hazel, who just looks at me and then down again.

"Do you play chess?" Sofia looks over at me as she slurps pasta.

"No," I say, shaking my head. "I tried to learn once. But it's just too hard for me."

Sofia puts her small hand on mine. "I can teach you," she tells me, and at that moment, I wonder if she knows how much of my heart she has. I wonder if she can feel the love that I feel for her. I don't give a shit that her hand is full of food and that now it's dirty. Her touch is everything. I look at the hand mark on mine. *I made that*, I think to myself. My whole life, I've been trying to make a mark on the world. My whole life, I tried to run away and be my own person. In the end, I helped create the perfect human being.

"I'll get you a rag," Hazel says, watching me just watch my hand. She jumps up now to grab a wet rag and hand it to me.

"I've been dirtier," I say, laughing as I grab the rag. She avoids my eyes with that comment and sits down.

After I finish my plate, I get up and help her clean up, trying to take in every minute I can. "I'm going to go and give her a bath," Hazel says. "You can wait or come back."

"I want to stay," I say honestly. "But I also want Sofia to be comfortable. When do you want me to come back?"

"After eight is good. She usually has a bath and then reads," she tells me. "She can read."

I smile proudly. "You did good, Hazel," I say softly, and I want to bring her to me and taste her lips. Just like I did all those years ago.

"Thank you," she says, looking away from me as if she heard my thoughts.

"Okay, Sofia," I say, walking over to her. "I'm going to go."

"Bye, Uncle Reed," she says. "Come back, and I can teach you chess."

I nod at them both and walk out of the house. I close the door behind me and sit on the stoop, putting my hands on my knees and letting my head hang.

I get up to leave, and I just can't. I sit down, my head turning around and around. The door opens, and I feel her come out and sit next to me. "You didn't leave." Her shoulder is against mine, and my whole body comes alive. "I looked out when I was putting the laundry in and saw your truck still here." I look over at her. Her hair is now tied on top of her head, little strands coming out.

"I meant what I said earlier," I say. "I'm not going anywhere."

She looks at me confused. "As long as you're here and Sofia is here, that is where I will be."

"I don't live here," she tells me.

"I know that," I say softly. "So wherever you will be, so will I."

"Reed," she says my name softly. "You don't have to do that."

"No." I shake my head. "I've lost five years of her life." I get up now and walk down the steps, turning to look at her. "Five years. First steps, first birthday, first day of school, first day she fell. I'm not missing another fucking second of her life." I want to kneel on the second step and hold her face in my hands while I tell her all of this.

"But you have a life," she says. "I don't expect you to give up everything that you have." She wipes the tear away. "You worked so hard to make it out of here."

"And I did that," I say. "I was supposed to sign another contract next month," I say now and see her face turn white. "I called my commander today and told them that I won't be doing it."

"But." She shakes her head.

"But nothing," I say. "For the first time in my life, I feel fucking whole. For the first time in my life, there is a reason to me." I point at myself. "For the first time in my life, I can breathe. Fuck, Hazel, I can't even explain to you how I feel. Because there are no words. The minute I found out that she was mine, everything." I shake my head and squat down so I can look her in her eyes. "Everything changed. That girl." I point at the window where I know she sleeps. "She owns me. So I'll move to wherever you live. I'll find a job, I'll bag groceries if I have to. I'll work for my father. I will do what I need to do to make sure that every single day I get to sit and be worthy of her love." I want to add both of you, but I know it has to be done in baby steps. "I can't imagine what you went through all alone without me." I blink the tears away, but they fall anyway. "And there is nothing I can say that will ever make it okay. Nothing." I swallow. "That is what I have to live with, but from now on, from this moment …" I put my hands on her cheeks now, holding her face in my palms. "You never have to go through this alone again. Not while I have air in my lungs."

"Reed," she says my name in a whisper, and it brings me back to six years ago when she whispered my name right before I slipped into her.

"Every single day," I say. "From this day on, it's going to be us. Me, you, and Sofia."

I want to lean in and kiss her, but instead, I drop my hands from her face and stand. I reach in the back of my pocket and take out the white envelope. "I don't have much," I say. "I've saved almost everything I've made over the years. I didn't need much to live."

"What are you talking about?" she says, and I hold out the envelope. "Take it, Hazel."

She takes the envelope and opens it, taking out the check for a hundred thousand dollars. She gasps out. "Are you insane?" she asks, shaking her head and putting the check back in the envelope. "I'm not taking this." She stands, pissed now. "Are you nuts?"

"You raised our daughter by yourself for the last five years. That isn't nearly enough to cover what you did." I turn now and walk toward my truck.

"I'm not taking this!" she yells at my back. "Stupid,

stubborn man."

I laugh now. "If you think I'm stubborn now." I open the truck door. "Wait until she tells me she wants to have a boyfriend."

"We need to talk about this," she tells me, putting her hands on her hips.

"We will." I take a second. "I haven't slept in two days, so I'm going home now, and I'm going to sleep." I step up in the truck. "See you tomorrow, Hazel."

"This isn't over, Reed Barnes," she says before she storms back into the house. When I hear her slam the door, I laugh.

"Damn fucking right, it's not over," I say while I drive away from them. The feeling of dread comes over me. I pick up the phone and call my brother, who answers after one ring.

"I'm putting the baby to bed," he says, whispering.

"Okay, just wanted to let you know that I need your help," I say. "Be at the barn at eight thirty tomorrow."

"Whatever," he says. "Just put a shirt on. Ethan posted a picture on Facebook of you riding a horse without a shirt, and I had to report it for profanity." I laugh now.

"I remember when you wore wifebeaters for a year," I remind him.

"I'm hanging up. Don't call me back," he says, disconnecting the call, and I call my father next, who answers right away also, but he's not whispering.

"Hey, Dad," I say. "I need a favor."

"Anything," he answers right away.

"Think you can meet me at the barn at eight thirty?"

I think about what to say. "I was over to see Hazel, and Sofia was out playing and she fell because the grass was too high." I close my eyes, hoping he doesn't sense the bullshit that I just gave him. "Since you just bought the house, I thought we could go over and at least clean it up a bit." I get out of the truck and make my way into the house, going straight to the bedroom.

"Yeah," he says. "That sounds good. I'll message the guys."

"Thanks, Dad," I say, and then he waits. "For everything."

"Anytime, son," he says, and for the first time, I get everything that he said. I hang up the phone and collapse into the bed. When I show up at the barn at eight thirty, every single man in my family is there, even Gabriel.

My grandfather is telling them what we are going to be doing, and everyone just listens.

"I've got the tractor already at the house," Grandpa says. "Let's roll, people."

"I'll ride with you," I tell my father, getting into his truck with Quinn, who leans his head against the headrest.

"Why the fuck are teeth so hard to cut through the gum?" he says, looking at my father.

"I'm not going to lie," my father says, driving toward Hazel's. "When you were getting your teeth in, I cried." I look at him in shock. "Seeing your kid in pain and not being able to help them is the fucking worst."

I lean forward now. "Did you cry?" I ask Quinn quietly, and he looks over his shoulder and shakes his head.

"Liar." My father laughs out louder. "You are a liar. I'm going to ask Willow." He parks the truck, and I see that even some of the ranch workers are here.

"I'm going to go and tell Hazel what is going on," I tell them. They both nod at me and walk into the field where my grandfather is now giving orders.

I'm walking to the front door when it opens, and Hazel comes out dressed in yoga pants and a shirt, followed by Sofia in overalls and her green Rubber boots. "Uncle Reed," she says.

"Hey, sunshine," I hear my grandfather say from beside me. "Hazel."

"Hi," she says. "What's going on here?" She looks around and sees all the men starting to work.

"Thought I would come by and give this little lady a ride on the tractor. What do you say?" my grandfather says. "If that is okay with your momma," he says, and the smile just fills my face when I see Sofia's eyes light up.

"Momma, a tractor," she says and looks over to the tractor and then walks to my grandfather.

"Let's go, sunshine," she tells him, and I can't help the laugh that escapes me.

Twenty

HAZEL

I WATCH IN disbelief as Sofia walks with Billy toward the tractor. "We shouldn't be here long," Casey says, looking at me. "But when we're done, she can run free." I don't say anything to him as he walks away.

"I thought I would be able to give you a warning," Reed says.

"A warning?" I ask, confused.

"I called the guys last night after I left here," he says. "I didn't think they would be so gung ho." He looks toward the field where everyone is working. "I'm going to go and make sure that Sofia likes me more than Grandpa," he says and turns to walk away but stops. "Oh, and you look beautiful today." He smirks at me and continues to walk to our daughter. His words cause my mouth to open and close.

"Don't go there, Hazel," I tell myself, turning and walking back into the house, going to the kitchen. I stand in front of the sink, looking out at the men in my yard.

"It's what they do." I hear Pops' voice in my head clear as day. "Family takes care of family." I swallow the sob, wishing he was here. Wishing he could see the day that Reed learned he was a father. I wish he could see how much he loves our little girl. I wish he would be here to sit on the porch with Billy as they talk about the little girl who holds a piece of both of them.

I see Billy on the tractor now with Sofia on his lap as he lets her pretend she's driving. The smile on her face is worth everything I have to go through. Being here isn't as much of a nightmare as I thought it would be.

Turning, I walk to the fridge and freezer. I take out stuff to make lunch for the men, but first, I start making my special chocolate chunk cookies. Ever since I got back home, I've been baking every single day, and I have to admit it's calmed me down when I thought I would be a nervous wreck.

I put the cookies on the tray and place them in the oven and then start making the chicken and cranberry sandwiches. I take out the three loaves of fresh bread I baked yesterday, and also get to making more sweet tea.

The door opens when I'm placing the sandwiches on a platter, and I look over to see Sofia running in. "Momma, I'm hungry," she says. She is covered in dirt, but nothing could tear me away from the sparkle in her eyes. "And I drive the tractor."

"Drove," I correct her. "Go wash your hands, and you can have some lunch," I say when the oven timer rings. Taking the cookies out, I place them on the stovetop to cool. "I'm going to go tell the boys to come in and eat," I say. "I'll be right back."

I walk toward where Casey and Billy stand as they look at Reed on the tractor. "I thought you guys might be hungry, so I made some sandwiches and sweet tea." I point with my thumb toward the house.

"You didn't have to," Billy says.

"Neither did you." I smile at him. "But here you are. It's the least I could do."

Billy smiles while Casey puts two fingers in his mouth and whistles. "Chomping time."

The guys drop what they're doing and follow me inside, and I realize how small the house is when the men have to sit half in the living room and half in the kitchen. "What is this?" Ethan takes a bite of the sandwich.

"Chicken salad with cranberry," I say.

"This is good," he says, taking another bite. I look around, making sure the men have food and are drinking.

"We did a lot," Reed says, standing next to me. "We should be done in a couple of hours."

"Can I drive the tractor again?" Sofia asks, and Billy nods.

The men thank me for lunch, and I almost forget the cookies. "Holy shit," Billy says and then looks over at Sofia. "Holy crap, these are amazing."

"Thank you," I say. "It's a secret recipe my great-grandmother had, and over the years, I've tweaked it just a touch."

"Well, it's perfect," he says. When they leave, there is not one piece of food left.

It takes them two more hours before they are finished. When Sofia comes in, I send her to the shower right away. I make more food than I should, and I'm somewhat hoping that Reed is going to come back so we can talk.

Sofia falls asleep practically at the table in her plate. I carry her to bed and think about if I should call him or not. I pace for a good ten minutes before calling. He answers right away, and I can tell that he was sleeping.

"I'm so sorry. Were you sleeping?" I ask, and I can hear the sheets rustling from his side.

"Shit," he says. "I wanted to come over to see Sofia."

"She fell asleep at the table. I'll let you go," I say. "We'll talk tomorrow."

"What did you make for dinner?" he asks, and I laugh.

"What difference does it make?" I sit on the couch, wondering where he's staying. Is he staying with his parents?

"So I know if I should eat before I come over." He laughs, and I can hear him walking.

"Sofia is in bed," I remind him.

"Yeah," he says, his voice soft. "I was wondering if we could talk." My stomach flips. "Go over a couple of things."

"Yeah," I say, my leg moving now. "We should talk about how things are going to go."

"Be there in ten," he says and disconnects. I get up now and make him a plate. I'm sure that he's hungry. I look at the phone in my hand, seeing the screen saver of Sofia and Pops staring back at me.

The nerves fill me now, and I have the sudden need to vomit. I put a hand to my stomach and walk to the kitchen, hanging my head. "It's going to be fine," I tell myself. "What is the worst that can happen?" I'm not helping anything at this point as my palms get sweaty.

I don't even have any time to talk myself out of it because I hear his truck arriving. I look at the door, waiting for the knock. It's going to be fine. Everything is going to be okay, and when I open it, I see him standing there, wearing dark blue jeans and a green shirt. His hair has been pushed back with his hands. I'm suddenly back to six years ago. The flutter in my stomach starts, and my heart speeds up. He always had this effect on me. "Hey," I say, stepping out of the way so he can come in. Everything is not fine. I should not be so attracted to him. It's been six years, six.

"Hey." He smiles, stepping in and coming straight to me, standing in front of me. I hold my breath as he comes closer and closer to me. His hand goes to my hip, and he leans in and kisses my cheek. "You look nice," he says, letting go of my hip. I'm wearing the same thing I was wearing this morning.

"You smell nice," I say and then close my eyes and wait for the floor to open up and swallow me whole.

"A shower will do that to you." He laughs, and I walk to the kitchen. "Smells amazing."

"I made meatloaf and mashed potatoes," I say, "with corn on the cob." I walk to the stove and pick up the plate. "Not sure if you stopped to eat or not." I grab a fork and knife and walk over to the table. "So I made you a plate."

He claps his hands together and sits down while I turn to grab him something to drink. "Did you eat?" he asks, and I nod.

"Yeah, we ate," I say and sit down in front of him.

"This is good," he says, eating, and I look at him.

"I was thinking," I start to say. "That we should go over a couple of things."

"I was thinking the same," he says between bites. "Sort of a can- and can't-do list."

"Yes." I nod at him. "If we are going to do this."

He looks up at me and smirks that fucking smirk I hate but love. "What are we going to do?" He puts down his fork. "I have a couple of things I'd like to do."

"What are you talking about?" I ask, confused. "I was talking about us co-parenting." He nods at me and continues eating his food. "Like I was saying, if we're going to do this, we need to have rules."

"I agree," he says.

"Routine," I start. "It's important that she stick to her routine." I swallow. "If she is at my house or at yours." The thought of her not being with me at night hits me, and I stop talking.

"Are you okay?" He looks up with concern on his face.

"Yeah," I say, blinking the tears away. "It's just she's always been with me, and now I'm going to have to …" Turning now, I get up to get myself some water. I feel him behind me as he puts his hands on my arms, his touch searing into my skin.

"One step at a time," he says softly. "One step at a time," he repeats, and I can feel the heat through my T-shirt now.

"Yeah," I say, afraid to turn around and come face-to-face with him because I'm not sure of myself right now. He drops his hands and steps away from me. Walking back to grab his plate, he rinses it off before he puts it in the dishwasher.

"Want to go sit outside?" he asks, and I nod. He grabs my hand and pulls me behind him, walking out of the house.

He sits down and pulls my hand so I sit next to him. "Relax, Hazel." He puts his hand over my shoulder. "You got this," he says. "Routine," he says. "We stick to her routine. I can do that." I nod. "I might need some help because, well, I don't know what the fuck I'm doing."

"Well." I look over at him. "I can tell you that you're doing a good job."

"If I fuck up, I am going to need you to tell me." I smile at him.

"Trust me, if you fuck up"—I smile big—"it will be my pleasure to tell you."

His hand drops from my shoulder now as he laughs out loud. "I've been in war zones," he says to me, his face looking out toward the trees. "And I'm more scared than I have been in my whole life." His voice trails off, and nothing could have prepared me for what is coming next.

Twenty-One

REED

I PUT MY hands on my knees, looking out in front of me. "What else is on your list?" I ask Hazel, looking at her.

"If I do something you don't like …" I look over at her again and fuck if she isn't as beautiful as she was all those nights ago. More beautiful than I remember, she is wearing another pair of yoga pants and a white T-shirt tucked into the front. The same thing she was wearing this morning, but seeing her again still takes my breath away. "Or if you do something I don't like, we talk to each other without Sofia."

"I would think that is a given," I say. "But I have no idea. I'll never put you down in front of her."

"Punishments," she says and holds her hands up. "I

don't spank her, never have had to. She's a great kid, and she is well behaved."

"She's the best," I say. "I know I'm biased, but in the two days I've known her, I can see how fucking amazing she is, and it's all because of you. I can't ever repay you." I stop talking, hoping I can say more, but I know I have to tread lightly. "I won't spank her." I shake my head, the thought making my stomach hurt.

"Fuck, when she told me she fell on that fucking rock …" I point at the field that we cleared today. "I swear on everything, I wanted to blow up the fucking rock with a bazooka." Hazel laughs now. "It's not funny. I had this rage in me." I shake my head. "Besides, I don't ever remember getting a spanking when we were growing up." I try to think back. "I don't think I ever got spanked." I laugh. "I mean, there were times I thought my father was going to ream my ass, but I sort of knew the tone." She nods her head, agreeing with me. "If my father said it in a certain tone, I knew if I fucked with him, he would have me over his knee. Remember when I crashed his car at fourteen." Her eyes open big now.

"Oh my God, I remember that," she says. "We didn't see you for a month."

"Because I mucked fucking stalls for a month from six a.m. until six p.m.," I say, laughing. "I even tried to go to summer school to get out of it, but nothing helped. At one point, my hand was stuck from holding a rake all day long."

She can't stop laughing, and I, for one, will listen to her laugh every single day of my life. Talking to her has always been so fucking easy. "But you never ever drove again until you got your license." She pushes my shoulder with her own. "Pops had a look, and I knew. He didn't give it to me often." She shakes her head now, most likely remembering that look. "I knew that it would be bad. All it took was a look, and I knew that whatever I was doing, I better fucking stop."

"I got that look once," I say, slapping my leg. "It was a Sunday barbecue. Christopher and I were chasing you. I think we were eleven or twelve. I couldn't catch you, so I pulled your bra strap from the back." I watch her to see if she remembers, but she just looks at me with her eyebrows pinched together. In the dark, I can't see her eyes, but when they sparkle, it's the best. "I turned to the side and saw Pops standing there, and I almost shit my pants from the look he gave me. I never touched another bra strap again. Plus, it didn't help that he was standing with Grandpa, and his look said that if Pops didn't kick my ass, he would." Her head goes back, and she laughs.

"Why can't I remember that?" she says.

"Fuck if I know," I say. "I thought I was going to piss myself there. I still remember Christopher almost shit himself. He never even looked at you twice. When you started working at the bar, he wouldn't even go near the tables you were working."

She gasps. "How did I never know this? I just thought he was quiet and shy."

I shake my head. "No, not even close."

"I guess we agree that if the other parent gives her a punishment, that we follow it when she is with them?"

she asks, and I nod. "Dating," she says, and I whip my head to look at her.

"Are you dating?" I ask, and my tone is harsher than I want it to be, but she caught me off guard. I guess it crossed my mind that maybe she had a man back home, but I was fucking hoping she didn't.

"I am not," she says. "I haven't dated in six years. It's pretty hard to date when you don't trust anyone with your daughter, and there are no family members to help out. Besides, it was hard to do it with a child," she says and all I can say is thank fuck. I look ahead, and neither of us says anything.

"It's crazy if you think about it," I start. "If I hadn't come home this time ..." I try not to think about it because it makes me want to throw up. "I would never know that I have a daughter." I can see that this bothers her. "I never thought I would be here," I say softly. "Do you know why I'm here?"

She shakes her head. "I haven't really kept up with what you have been doing. Besides Pops, I never really talked to anyone here. He brought you up the first two years, and he knew that I just couldn't even handle hearing your name. I was so hurt that you didn't even answer my message. He tried to talk me into coming home and telling Billy and Charlotte, but ..." She takes a deep breath. "I wasn't going to give them the burden of Sofia or me. So I worked harder to make sure that she was never ever missing anything."

My heart breaks again, knowing she went through all of this by herself. I owe her more than what I can give her. “This is the first time in six years I’ve been back,” I say, and she gasps in shock.

“I knew you wanted to leave,” she says. “But I always thought you would come back to visit.”

I shake my head. “Just the thought of coming back here would make me sick,” I say the truth. “I would sign up for another deployment just to escape from coming back here.”

“Then why now?” she asks, and I swallow.

“When I left here,” I start, “it was so fucking liberating. I was in no one’s shadow. I was just Reed Barnes,” I say. “The first month was fucking awesome. Highest on the scoreboard. Beat my records, and not one person mentioned my father or my brother.” She just listens and doesn’t say anything. “The second month was going well and then I fucking missed them,” I admit to her and to myself for the first time ever. “I missed seeing them, being with them. Then I got your message.” I shake my head. “It fucking threw me off the track.” She blinks away her own tears now. “I’m so sorry I never answered you, and until I die, that will be my biggest regret. But I had to cut the ties. It fucked me up for a week.” My hand comes out. “I never came back because I knew that if I did, I wouldn’t have the balls to leave again. So whenever I had leave, I traveled. Picked a spot and backpacked.”

“So why are you here now?” she asks.

“Eight weeks ago …” I close my eyes, and I can see it like it’s happening right now in front of me. “My squad and I were taking a drive to the city.” I swallow, and I can feel the heat on my body. "Routine. Nothing out of the ordinary. I heard the whizzing before I had a chance to do anything. I was in charge of the squad, and all I could do was yell *incoming*." The pain in my chest is just as intense as it was that day. "It gave the driver a split second to swerve before a missile hit us." Her hand goes to her chest. "I blinked, and all I saw was black. I don't remember anything. I heard screaming. When I opened my eyes, there was this buzzing noise, and it took me a second to realize where I was. I had glass all over me, and I will never forget the smell of burnt flesh." She puts her hand on my leg now, the exact leg that was stuck. "I was stuck," I say. "I was under a part of the truck, and I could hear the bullets trying to hit us. I raised my head, and all I saw was dust everywhere. I reached for my radio, but I just couldn't grasp it. I yelled for my men, and we were all in bad shape. But their lives rested on my shoulders."

"You were trapped," she says in a whisper.

"I felt the steel in my leg." I look down to where her hand is, and she takes it off as if my leg is on fire. "I knew that if I didn't get out of there, I would die there." She wipes the tears running down her face. "I knew that if I gave up and waited for help, they would take us, and we would be their fucking pawn." I shake my head, my voice cracking. "That wasn't happening. Not on my watch."

"What did you do?" she whispers.

"I closed my eyes and shut everything down and pulled my leg free. I felt the steel rip through my flesh.

The burning went right down to my bones. But I got the radio and got an air strike to come and rescue us. I pulled two of the guys who had burns on their hands to safety, and it was the longest twenty-two minutes of my life. The minute I got into the helicopter, I faded to black. I woke up seven days later in Germany. I was put on the injury list, thirty days until my next check-in, so I called my father and decided to come home. Fuck." I shake my head. "I always wondered why I didn't die there that day. I wondered why I was saved, but now being here, coming home, I know why." My own tears stream down my face. "It was for you, this." I look into her eyes. "It was for you two."

Twenty-Two

HAZEL

I LISTEN TO him say his story, and the whole time, my heart is in my throat. The whole time, I thank whoever is listening for saving him. "I'm so sorry," I say, and my hand comes up to cup his cheek. "For not pushing to get in touch with you sooner. I should have contacted your parents." The lump in my throat is as big as a baseball, and I want to say so many words, but I don't trust myself right now.

"How were you supposed to know?" he says.

"What if something would have happened to you and you died not knowing?" I try to control the sob that wants to rip through me. "I'm so sorry." His head turns to kiss the palm of my hand on his cheek.

"I think it's safe to say we both fucked up and made

mistakes," he says softly, putting his hand over mine. "The good news is that we now know." He looks in my eyes, and I want to lean in and kiss his lips. He's the last person I've ever kissed. He's the only kiss that I remember, and he's the only kiss that I dream of.

I smile through my tears at him. "I'm really glad you didn't die." He laughs, his hand falling off mine and my hand falling to his leg. The moment's suddenly gone, and I wonder if he did it on purpose. If kissing me is not what he wants to do. I know he said that he hasn't dated, but he could still have someone in his life.

"I'm really glad I didn't die either," he says, getting up now. "I'm really fucking glad I didn't die." He walks down the step. "And I'm really fucking glad I came home." He looks at me. "See you in the morning," he says. "Lock up."

"I will." I get up and turn to walk back into the house. When I hear the sound of the rocks crunching as he pulls out of the driveway, I lock the door. Walking to the kitchen, I clean up before heading up to bed. I watch Sofia sleep for a while before sleep comes and takes me.

"Momma." I hear a soft voice. "Uncle Reed is here." My eyes spring open, and I sit up in bed, the cover falling off me.

"What?" I look at Sofia in confusion, then turn to grab the phone on the side table. I see it's past seven, but there are five texts, all from Reed.

Reed: It's me. I got up early.

Reed: I'll be there by seven.

Reed: Is it okay if I come over?

Reed: Heading that way now.

Reed: I'm outside.

"It's fine." I look over and see him standing in the doorway. He leans against the doorjamb, wearing jeans and a T-shirt. His hair looks like he just got out of the shower. "I knocked and thought you were up." He smirks as he looks at me and then down at the floor.

Looking down, I see my nipples are peeking out. My hand flies to grab the cover, and I bring it to my chest. "I didn't hear you wake up." I look over at Sofia, who is getting off the bed. "I didn't even hear you knock."

"I heard it, Momma," Sofia says, walking to Reed and slipping her hand in his.

"You opened the door?" I shriek out. "Sofia Bernadette," I say her name.

"She did," Reed says, and I don't know if he's protecting her or not. "She asked who it was. Then she said you were sleeping." He looks down at her, smiling. "Then she opened the door when I said it was me."

"Are you going to make pancakes, Momma?" Sofia asks and doesn't even give me a chance to answer. "Uncle Reed, can you make pancakes? I'm hungry."

"I can make pancakes," he says to her, bending and picking her up. "But I don't think they are as good as your momma's." He looks at me now. "Why don't we go down and I can cut some fruit, and Momma can get dressed?" She nods her head. "Not that I mind what you're wearing." He winks. "But there might be other things happening we would need to explain."

I just look over at him, and my eyebrows pull together.

He looks down at his jeans, seeing that his cock is awake, and my eyes go big. "I'll be right down in clothes." He laughs, kissing Sofia's head, and turns to walk out of the room. I get up and grab some shorts. I usually sleep in panties and a tank top. I can hear him and Sofia talking downstairs while I wash my face in the bathroom. I grab a sweater and put it over my tank top, and walk downstairs, the smell of coffee filling the room.

Sofia sits on the counter next to him as he cuts an apple for her. "You cut it the other way." She gives him instructions. "Sometimes Momma puts apple in my oatmeal," she tells him. "But you need to cut it small so I don't choke."

"I'll remember that," he says. "Now, do you want strawberries and banana?"

"Yes, please," she says, smiling at him.

"Coffee?" I ask, and he just nods. "How do you take it?" I grab two cups of coffee, filling them.

"It doesn't matter," he says, and I just look over at him and tilt my head. "Fine, milk, please."

I walk to the fridge, grabbing the milk and splashing a bit in both of them. "Do you take sugar?"

"Nope," he says. Putting the knife down, he grabs Sofia and carries her to the chair. "I'm sweet enough." He kisses her nose, and I roll my eyes. He walks back to the counter, grabbing the fruit plate he made for her and bringing it to her.

"Here you go." I hand him the cup of coffee. His hand grazes mine while he grabs his cup, making my heart speed up with just his touch.

"I'll start the pancakes," I say, expecting him to get out of the kitchen. Instead, he stands at the far end of the kitchen, leaning back on the counter.

"Is there anything I can do to help?" he asks, and I look over at him while I whisk the dry ingredients.

"You can get me two eggs," I say. He pulls open the fridge and comes back to give me the two eggs.

"Thank you," I say, grabbing the eggs and cracking them into a bowl but only using the egg whites.

"What do you have planned today?" Reed asks.

"I have to run into town for a couple of things." I look at him as I get the egg whites just perfect. "There are some papers at the bank that I need to file for Pops." I make sure the griddle is the right temperature before scooping some batter on there. I add the oil and a little bit of butter for the richness.

"Actually." I look over at him once I put six scoops of batter. "Would you be able to watch Sofia?" He smiles. "I just figure she'd have a better time with you doing anything else but getting in the car and going for meetings."

"Well." He looks over at Sofia. "I did buy something she might like." Her eyes light up, and I look over at him.

She claps her hands together. "Is it a tractor?" she asks, and I shake my head and laugh quietly.

"It is not a tractor," he tells her. "But I'm sure you'll love it."

"What did you buy her?" I ask, and he ignores the question when he brings the coffee cup to his lips to hide his smile, but I can tell from the crinkles around his eyes that it's a full-face smile.

"I'll get you plates," he says, turning and grabbing three plates. He walks to me, one hand going to my hip while he puts the plates down beside me. "You smell good," he says, burying his face in my hair.

"It's the pancakes," I say, trying to make it so he doesn't know that my pulse has sped up with his touch. I try to make sure my chest rises and falls naturally and not pant.

"It's not the pancakes," he says, walking away from me now and going to sit in the chair next to Sofia.

I put one pancake on Sofia's plate and another one on mine and stack three on his, leaving one on the counter in case he or Sofia want more.

"I got to give it to you, Hazel," Reed says after he finishes the three on his plate, the one on the counter, and the rest of Sofia's. "You can cook."

I shrug my shoulders, and I'm getting up to clean the dishes when he stops me. "I've got the kitchen. Go get ready."

"Well, then, you won't hear me argue." I grab another cup of coffee and head upstairs. I slip on my tight jeans and a white button-down shirt, rolling up the sleeves and tucking it in the front. After slipping on my tan ballerina shoes, I comb my hair and put on some mascara. I take more time than I care to admit on my appearance. When I walk downstairs, I see that the kitchen is almost done.

"Her clothes are on the bed," I say. He looks over his shoulder, and his hand stops in the water. He takes his hand out and grabs the hand towel, drying it off and placing it over his shoulder. "I shouldn't be long." I get nervous now as he just watches me. "Is everything okay?"

"Yeah," he says, his voice low. "I'm just … you're stunning." I try not to let his words get to me. "I'm going to have a hard time when Sofia gets older if she looks anything like her momma."

I turn away from his look, not ready for him to see that I'm blushing. "Give Momma a kiss," I tell Sofia who just colors. She looks up at me, and I kiss her on her lips. "Be good for—" I almost slip and say dad. "Be good."

"Do I get a goodbye kiss?" Reed asks, and I roll my eyes, grabbing my purse and almost running out of the house. I put my hand on my head once I'm sitting in my car, trying to get all the butterflies out of my stomach.

"Motherfucker," I say to myself. "Falling for Reed Barnes is a stupid idea, Hazel." I drive out of the driveway and toward town. I get out of the truck, and I'm walking when I see four women walking toward me. One of them is heavily pregnant.

"There she is," Amelia says as she waddles toward me. Chelsea is beside her with Savannah on one side and Kallie on the other side. "You have some explaining to do."

I put my hand to my chest, and I wonder if Reed told his family, my hands starting to shake and my mouth goes dry. "Sorry."

"Don't sorry me," Amelia says. "I heard you made the best blueberry scones alive, and Auntie Savannah just gave me the last one."

The relief goes out of me, and I laugh. “We aren’t even going to discuss the sandwiches that my husband now wants me to make,” Chelsea says. “Chicken and cranberry.” She shakes her head.

“Leave her alone,” Savannah says, coming to my side.

“I’m going to get her to the diner,” Kallie says, putting her hand around Amelia’s shoulders. “Before she gets really hangry and shows up at your door.”

“I can get you some scones,” I say, and her eyes light up. “I’ll make them tonight.”

“See you tomorrow,” she says, walking around me. “Or today if you finish them and want to drive them over to me.”

“I’ll see,” I say and then turn back to see Savannah.

“I was hoping I would see you out,” she says. “Do you have a couple of minutes?” she asks.

“I do,” I say, and she smiles.

“Follow me,” she says, and I walk with her across the small parking lot to the vacant new stores I saw when I was driving into town. She takes the keys out of her pocket and opens the door.

I walk in and see an empty space, the big windows in the front allowing the sun to come in. “Now, before you say anything,” she tells me, “I want you to picture a long wooden counter on this side.” She points at the side of the room. “With a huge display case in the back.” I turn, watching her walk across the room. “Wooden beams everywhere, and I want it to be like your grandmother’s kitchen,” she tells me. “I’d love to put a couch in the back of that corner for when people come in and there are more than six." She smiles now, her eyes lighting up. "A homey feel. There are going to be little round tables everywhere. I was thinking we can have coffee cups for sale in a wooden hutch."

"I think it would be amazing," I say honestly. "You are going to get the older crowd, and also you might even touch the younger kids in high school who want to come and just get some chill time." I shake my head. "I think you have an amazing idea."

"Good," she says. "I need a partner." I'm about to tell her something, and she puts her hand up. "I don't know how to bake, but I know how to run a business."

"I don't know how to bake," I say. "All these things are just—"

"It's a talent you can't teach." She laughs. "Do you know how many times Charlotte tried to teach me how to make apple pie because it was Ethan's favorite?" She puts her hands on her hips. "And Olivia, she's started more kitchen fires than she cares to admit."

"It's just … I don't," I start to say. "I don't live here." Also, I think of the money I have in my savings that I don't want to dip into.

"You can change that," she tells me. "I'll put up all the capital, but we would still be fifty-fifty partners."

"Um," I start to say.

"I'll take back five percent yearly until it's all paid back," she says.

"What if it doesn't make it back?" I ask her. "What if you invest all this money and it's a flop?"

"Oh …" She shakes her head. "Ye have little faith." She looks around now. "Ye have little faith."

Twenty-Three

Reed

“READY?” I ASK Sofia as she puts on her Rubber boots. After Hazel left, I finished cleaning the kitchen while Sofia colored. She made sure to tell me what needed to be done. I was just the adult supervisor. She got dressed and made sure she brushed her teeth before walking down the stairs.

“Ready, Freddy,” she says, turning to look at me. She slips her hand in mine, and I walk out of the house and open the back door to the truck. “Where is my seat?” she asks, and I look at her. “I need a booster seat,” she tells me, “or else I’ll fly out of the car and die.” I almost laugh because I can see Hazel telling her that.

“I don’t have one. But we can walk over to my house,” I say. “And then take the golf cart to Grandpa’s.” I look at her, waiting for her to okay this plan.

We start walking toward my house. "You have a house here?" she asks.

"Not really," I say. "It's my mom and dad's." I look over at her as we walk, her little legs moving fast.

"We don't live here either," she tells me. "We live in a condo."

"Do you like living in a condo?" I ask, trying not to laugh that she knows that word.

"It's okay. Sometimes we go to the beach," she tells me, and you can tell from her voice that she's excited about the beach. She goes on and on about how she swims and that she took swimming at home. When we make it to my house, she looks up at the house. "You live in a big house." She looks around and walks toward the golf cart.

I pick her up and set her down, then get into the driver's seat. I put my hand over her hand when I start to drive. She looks around, and when we get closer to the barn, she starts to fidget in the seat. When I stop the golf cart, she squeals out in excitement. "Are we going to ride horses?" she asks, and I can tell she likes the horses better than the beach.

"I think we can," I say, getting out of the golf cart and holding out my hand for her. She grabs my hand, and we walk into the barn. She walks past the stalls, and I stop at the stall where her horse is in. "What do you think of this one?" I ask, and the horse comes toward us. I pick her up in my arms as the horse sticks her snout out of the stall.

"She's pretty," Sofia says, and she follows my lead

when I rub the horse's snout.

"Well, well, well." I look over to see my grandfather coming toward us. "If it isn't the prettiest girl I've ever seen." He stops in front of us. Sofia just smiles at him as she rubs the horse.

"Uncle Reed said we can ride horses," she informs him, and he just nods his head.

"Is that so?" he says, putting his hands on his hips. "This is interesting," he says, and I just look over at him. Sofia is not even noticing what he's saying.

"Hazel asked me to watch her." I avoid looking into his eyes. Instead, I watch Sofia. "We were friends before I left." I look at him and see the questions in his eyes. "It's fine."

He just nods. "So are we going to saddle her?" he asks me, and Sofia just puts her hands together and laughs.

"I think that's a yes." She smiles and nods her head. I put her down now. "Don't move," I say, walking over to the wall and grabbing a saddle. I keep one eye on her the whole time, making sure she's okay. "Now," I say, walking to her. "We are going to saddle her so we can take her out."

She jumps up and down now as I walk into the stall. "This is better than the tractor," she says and then looks up at my grandfather. "I still like the tractor." She tries not to hurt his feelings, making him laugh.

"Now you are going to behave," I tell the horse once I throw the saddle on her back. "And you are going to be gentle with her or else," I whisper to her, and the horse looks at me as if she knows what I'm saying. "No funny tricks."

"Is it ready?" Sofia asks, and I look at her and walk out with the horse. Grandpa places her behind him in case the horse bucks or kicks her.

"She's pretty," Sofia says as we walk out. She walks over and slips her hand in mine. "What's her name?"

"I don't know," I say as we walk toward the fenced area. "What do you think we should call her?"

"Caramel," she says. "'Cause she looks like the caramel candies Momma gives me."

"That's a perfect name," my grandfather says.

"Let's go," I say, walking into the fenced area with her. "I'm going to put you on, and I want you to hold on tight," I say. She raises her arms for me to pick her up and put her on the horse. "You good?" I ask her, and she holds the front of the saddle, smiling. "Now I'm going to walk her around, okay?" I walk her around two times, and by the third time, I can tell that she wants to pick up the pace. She is my daughter, after all. I never was one to have patience.

"I knew I'd find you here." I look behind me to see my father coming in. He's dressed in jeans and a shirt, his hands filthy. "Is that the new horse?"

"She's Caramel," Sofia says to my father, and she smirks at him. He looks up at her, smiling and then looks back at me.

"I'll take her out there," my grandfather says, taking the reins from me. "Let's go and work her out."

"Not too fast," I tell my grandfather, and he just smiles at me.

I watch my grandfather walk the area with Sofia as he explains things. "Son." I hear my father. "Is there something you need to tell me?" he asks, and I wonder if he noticed that she smiles like me.

"I don't know what you mean," I say, avoiding his eyes. "I'm helping Hazel." The lie eats at my stomach. I hate lying, always have. But then to lie about what she is to me, that is just … I fucking hate it. There are no other words to describe it.

"You haven't been around kids," he says as we stand against the fence watching.

"She's five," I say. "She is basically babysitting me."

"She's a natural," my father says, watching Sofia on the horse now after my grandfather handed her the reins.

"Must be the country girl in her," I say, walking into the area before my father asks more questions. I have to walk away from him before I lie to him.

"I can gallop," Sofia tells me, smiling. "Can we go fast now?" I look over at my grandfather, who shakes his head.

"She's been asking me this for the last ten minutes," he says.

"Okay," I say, putting my foot in the stirrup and getting on the horse with her. "Why don't we take her out?"

"See you two later," he says, walking to my father. Both of them watch me. I lock her in and start for the trail when my phone rings.

"Hello," I say when I answer it.

"Hey." I hear Hazel's voice, and a smile fills my face.

"It's me."

"Hi, it's me," I joke with her, and she laughs.

"Where are you guys?" she asks, and I hear the car door shut.

"Going for a ride," I say. "Sofia named my horse."

"Oh, good God," Hazel says, laughing. "Do I want to know?"

"I'll let her tell you," I say as we ride out of the area.

"Well, if it's okay with you, I'm going to go home and bake Amelia some scones, and then I'll come by and get her," she says.

"Yeah, that's fine," I say. "I'm going to take her for a ride anyway."

"Um, okay," she says, hesitating. "If you need anything …"

"I'll call," I say. "See you later, Hazel." I hang up now and get up to tuck the phone in my pocket. "Okay, you ready?" I say, and she just smiles up at me and nods her head. I kick the horse with the side of my foot. "Get," I say, and she opens up and races. The whole time, I have Sofia in my arms. I ride until I can feel Caramel is tired, and the sun is soaking through my T-shirt. I pull it over my head now. "We are going to need a shower after this." I look down at Sofia, whose eyes sparkle with happiness. "Let's get back and see if Grandma will give us something to drink and a snack. My favorite is chocolate chip muffins."

"Me, too," she says, and I throw my head back and laugh, pretty sure that she would have said anything was her favorite.

"Let's go," I tell the horse.

"Caramel, take me home," she says and mimics my kick on the side.

"You really are a natural." I kiss the top of her head as she leads us back to the barn.

Pulling up, I see her right away. She stands there with a basket over her arm as she talks to my grandfather, and he eats whatever is in the basket. She looks over and puts her hand over her eyes to see us without the sun blinding her.

"There they are," I hear my grandfather tell her. "Thank you for the scone."

"It's my pleasure," she says and looks back at us. "Why are you not wearing a shirt?" she asks when I get closer to her. The sound of my grandfather's laughter fills the air.

"He's trying to be your Romeo." He winks at Hazel, and she rolls her lips as he walks away now.

"Momma, I rode Caramel," Sofia says. "Fast fast."

"Did you?" Hazel says, and I get down from the horse and then reach for Sofia as she leans to me. "Was it fun?" Sofia shakes her head, and I see my grandfather opening the fence.

"Let's go get her some water," my grandfather says, holding out his hand for Sofia and then the other hand for the reins.

Grabbing my shirt, I put it over my shoulder as I walk closer to her. I can tell that she has mischief all over her face, and when she opens her mouth, I know why. "What's up, Romeo?"

Twenty-Four

Hazel

"WHAT'S UP, ROMEO?" I joke with him and throw my head back when he groans out.

"It was hot out there," he says, and I look at him with his shirt off. He's definitely filled out since the last time. A scar on the lower right side of his stomach has my eyes lingering there. My fingers itch to touch it.

"Momma." I hear my name being called and turn to see Sofia running out of the barn. Her overalls are dusty, and her Rubber boots are wet. "I gave Caramel water," she says, and the smile on her face makes her eyes a light brown almost green. "Now Grandpa Billy says I can feed her," she tells me and then turns to run back into the barn.

"I don't think she's been this excited in her whole life," I say, turning now and seeing that Reed is standing really close to me. I can smell his musky woodsy smell. "Today was good?" I ask, pretending that standing this close to him does nothing for me. Meanwhile, I want to lean into him and slide my tongue into his mouth.

"It was great," he says, looking at me and then the barn where Sofia just ran into. "It's crazy how it's so natural with us."

I smile at him. "I don't think I've seen her this happy."

"Did you get all your errands done?" he asks, and I nod.

"I did, and then I saw your aunts and Amelia and Chelsea." I leave out the conversation I had with Savannah.

"What's in the basket?" His eyes glimmer just like Sofia's, the smirk on his face making him dangerous.

All the words leave my head as I watch him stick out his tongue and lick his lower lip. "Um," I say, clearing my throat and blinking my eyes to get myself out of the daze. "I made some blueberry scones, and then I had some orange and cranberry, so I made those scones also."

"Ohh," he says, his hands going for my basket.

"Don't you dare touch my scones with your dirty hands, Mr. Romeo," I say, laughing and then see his eyes turn a darker brown.

"If I can't touch your scones with my dirty hands," he says and steps closer to me. "What can I touch?" It's my turn to stick my tongue out of my mouth and lick my lips. My stomach tightens, shooting sensations all the way down to my toes.\

"Momma," Sofia says, running back to me. "I'm

done." Reed takes a step back now. "Can we go eat?"

"Sure," I say, holding out my hand and then handing Reed the basket. "Those are for you."

"For me?" he asks, shocked.

"It's the least I could do for helping today," I say, and he smiles.

"Hopefully, we can do it again." He looks at me, and I just nod.

"Let's get you home and in the bath." I swing our hands. "Say thank you."

"Thank you, Uncle Reed," she says, pulling from my hand and walking to him to wrap her little arms around his waist. "It was the bestest day ever."

He blinks away the tears in his eyes, squatting down in front of her when she lets him go. "It was my bestest day ever." He taps her nose with his finger. "I'll see you later." He gets up when she turns and runs to me.

"I'm making chicken potpie for dinner," I say over my shoulder when I walk away. "There may be a serving for you." He smirks.

"I'll see you soon, then." He watches us get into the truck, and only when we drive away do I see him walk back into the barn.

"So how was your day?" I ask her, looking into the rearview mirror.

"We had so much fun," she says with her hands raising up in the air. "I rode Caramel by myself," she tells me. "And then I wanted to go fast fast." Her voice is so full of life I can't help but smile with her. "So Uncle Reed came on the horse with me, and we went super-duper fastest," she says, clapping her hands.

I pull up to the house, and she's already out of her car seat and jumps out of the truck when I open the back door. "In the shower," I say as I open the door, and she nods at me while she kicks off her Rubber boots. I kick off my ballerina shoes and follow her up the stairs to the bathroom while she is going on and on about Caramel. I start the shower for her and then walk back to the bedroom and pick up some shorts and a shirt for her.

Dressing her and combing out her hair, I braid it for her, and she asks to go sit on the couch to watch television. I set her up and walk back to the kitchen, putting the chicken potpie into the oven to bake.

"Momma!" I hear her yell my name. "Do you think Caramel is going to miss me?"

"Yes," I say, smiling. "But I'm sure she'll be fine."

"Stay here and build something amazing with me." I can hear Savannah's voice in my head. I couldn't even say a word to her when she told me that. All I could see is getting up every day and walking into the shop, greeting people who I knew when I was a little girl. It was the whole reason I wanted out of this town, but now having Sofia here, I wonder how much she would flourish living here. Seeing her at the barbecue with the kids was everything. Seeing her with Billy and Charlotte was enough to make me burst into tears. They love her, and they don't even know that she's theirs.

My mind lingers, trying to think back to when we are at home. Surely, there was a time when she was as happy as she is here.

She has never smiled as much as she has here. Coming here, I knew it would be hard on me, but even I have had more smiles than I think I did at home. Don't get me wrong, I love my life. I love our life. But after being here for three weeks, I have to admit something was missing.

I was going through the motions every single day, but I was empty inside. It was a routine—wash, rinse, repeat. I would go to work because that was my job, but I wasn't over-the-moon excited to be there. In my head, that was how it was supposed to be. No one really loves what they do every single day.

Cutting the lettuce and then tossing it into the bowl, I think of the last time I woke up with a sense of dread. I haven't had to force one smile since I've been here. It's all been natural. I haven't had to give myself pep talks either or bribe Sofia once to do anything.

The knock on the door has me turning, and Sofia gets up, looking at me. "Can I open the door?" I nod at her, thinking that I would have put her behind me back home and walked to the door to see who it was before I even thought of opening it.

She turns the handle of the door, and it's not even locked. "Uncle Reed," she says, and I look over at him as he stands there with two bouquets.

"I brought you flowers," he tells her, and her eyes open wide. "From Caramel and me." He hands her the small bouquet of daisies.

She takes it and walks to me with it. "I got flowers," she tells me, and I put my hands on my hips.

"Isn't that special?" I tell her, and then she hands it to

me, turning and walking back to the television.

I look over at Reed, who just stares at me and then comes in. “Somehow, in my head, that was going to have more fanfare than it just did.” I laugh at him now. “She was happier giving Caramel water.”

“I’m sure she loved them both the same.” I try to make him feel better.

“These are for you,” he says, handing me the bigger bouquet.

“You shouldn’t have,” I say, not even trying to hide the smile. “I’ve never gotten flowers before,” I say, turning to search for a vase. “Thank you, that was very sweet of you.”

He puts his hands in the back pockets of his jeans, and I look at him, tilting my head to the side. “Is everything okay?” I ask, and he looks at the television now and then Sofia before turning back and looking at me.

“Yeah,” he says, and I sense he’s trying to say something. “We need to talk,” he says. “But not now, when she goes to bed.”

That has to be the worst thing you could say to me right now. My stomach sinks, and I just nod at him as so many things go through my head. Maybe he spent the day with her, and he decided that it’s not for him. Maybe he’s just not cut out for this. It’s fine. It will be fine, I tell myself. “Yeah, sure,” I say, avoiding looking at him. I put the vase on the counter and fill it with water. “Dinner is almost done,” I say, and he just leans on the counter and looks at me.

“Is everything okay?” he asks, and I just look over at

him.

"Yeah," I say, ignoring even looking at him. I can feel him staring at me, and my nerves get the best of me. "Listen, I don't know what you want to talk to me about," I say, looking at him and then at Sofia again. "But if you don't want to do this." I motion with my hand in a circle. "It's okay."

"Hazel, I've never been more sure of doing this in my whole life," he says, not moving from the counter. "In fact, this …" He motions with his own hand in a circle, and the look he gives me is making my mouth go dry and my hands shaky. "Is just the beginning."

Twenty-Five

Reed

I WATCH HER eyes when I say the words. "In fact, this …" I mimic her when I put my hand in a circle, my eyes staring into hers. "Is just the beginning." She swallows, and I force myself not to go to her and take her in my arms. It's taking everything not to take her face in my hands and kiss the ever-loving shit out of her. "Just so we are on the same page." She nods. I turn my head to look at Sofia, seeing that her eyes are getting heavy. "Sofia." I call her name, and she looks over, and I can tell she's exhausted. "Want to help me set the table?"

She gets off the couch and comes over, rubbing her eyes. I lean down and pick her up. "Tired, baby girl?" I ask softly. She puts her head on my shoulder, and I thought I would be ready for this. I thought I had all of this wrapped up in my head. I knew I loved her with every single fiber of my being. I knew I wanted to be her father with everything I had in me. But now I know that I would die before I bring even one ounce of pain to her.

"Yeah," she says softly. "Can we go see Caramel tomorrow?" she asks, and I look over at Hazel, who is wiping a tear away from her face.

"Anything," I tell Sofia, who perks up and squirms to get out of my arms. She walks over and grabs the forks out of the drawer.

"That," Hazel says, "is her wrapping you around her tiny little finger." I can't even answer her because she's right.

Dinner goes off smooth again, and when it's time to clean the dishes, Sofia looks at Hazel. "Can Uncle Reed say my prayers with me?" My eyes go from her to Hazel, who smiles, my heart exploding in my chest.

"Sure," Hazel says, getting up now and taking the plates. "I'll clean up here."

Sofia slips her hand in mine, and we walk up the stairs together. She grabs her nightgown and shows me her whole nightly routine. She climbs into bed after she brushes her teeth. "Now you read me a story," she tells me, and I pick up a book from the side table. "Not that one," she tells me, and I laugh. "The pink one."

"Okay," I say, picking up the pink book and reading it to her. She yawns and turns on her side when I finish. She says her prayer, and when she thanks God for Caramel and me, I don't think I can get up and walk. I lean down and kiss her cheek. "I love you, baby girl," I say, and her eyes close. I stay up here so long that I hear the stairs creak and look over at Hazel.

"Is everything okay?" she asks and looks at the bed, seeing Sofia sleeping peacefully.

"She thanked God for me," I say, my voice trembling. "She's …" I shake my head, trying to get the words out. "She's fucking incredible."

"She is." She smiles, leaning into the doorframe. "She's lucky to have you as a father."

I look down at the floor. "I want to tell my parents," I say. "That's what I wanted to talk to you about." I look back at the little girl lying in bed. "Fuck, I want to tell the world."

She just looks at me. "Before we tell the world," she says, "we need to tell her." She points at Sofia. "Why don't you tell your parents and then we can tell her after?"

"I'm not joking about this, Hazel," I say, and she just looks at me. "I'm going to tell them tomorrow. I'm not waiting, watching everyone love her from afar." I swallow. "It's not fair to them." I get up now and walk to her. Standing in front of her, I lift my fingers and touch her cheek. "I'll come over after I talk to my parents," I say. She looks at me and swallows. "Sleep tight, Hazel." I lean in and kiss the corner of her mouth and her cheek. I turn around before I press her against the door.

Going down the stairs, I'm hoping she stops me from walking out the door. I close the door behind me. "All in good time." I barely sleep that night with the phone in my hand, and at seven, I call my father.

"This is early," he says, laughing.

"Yeah, do you think I can come over and talk to you and Mom?" I ask, and my father stops laughing.

"We're home now if you—" he says, and I cut him off.

"Okay, I'll be there in ten," I say and hang up the phone. I walk out the door wearing shorts and a T-shirt. When I got up this morning, I dressed to go to the gym, but the only thing I could do was go over my speech for my parents. I pull up to the house that I grew up in and see a little tricycle on the side of the house, and I know it's for Quinn's baby girl. I get out now. My heart is pounding in my chest so hard I stop walking, and I bend down, afraid I'm going to be sick. I don't think I can handle it if they don't accept her. I know they will, but the thought of them being mad or upset about it, makes me sick to my stomach.

The front door opens and my father comes out of the house. He stops when he sees me. "I'm fine," I say, lifting my hand. My father waits for me at the door with worry all over his face, and when I walk up to him, I give him the biggest hug I've ever given him in my whole life. "Hey, Dad," I say, trying to compose myself. He lets me go and puts his hand on my neck, his eyes on mine.

"Hey, son." He squeezes me, and we walk into the house. I can hear pots banging from the kitchen.

The pictures all over the wall have me stopping for a second when I know that my daughter's is going to be up there. Walking into the kitchen, my mother looks over at me and stops moving. "What happened?" She puts the pot down. "Who died?"

I shake my head. "No one died," I say, and she just looks over at my father for guidance. "I wanted to sit down with you guys," I say, and my mother walks over to me. "Can we sit?" I walk over to the living room and sit down.

They sit down in front of me. My mother already has tears streaming down her face as my father puts his arm around her. "Jesus," I say, getting up now. "I thought this would be easier."

"Okay," my father says. "You have three seconds to calm the fuck down," he says, knowing I need him to be strong with me. "Whatever it is."

I stop and look at them. I think of different ways to start the conversation and different ways to say it, but in the end, it leads back to one thing. "I have a daughter," I tell them, and I see my mother put her hands to her mouth.

"You have a daughter?" my father asks. "Or you're having a daughter?" He leans back into the chair.

"I have a daughter," I tell them, and my mother gasps out. "She's five." My father looks at me, not saying a word. "You've met her."

"Sofia," my father says, and my mother gasps out when I nod my head.

"I didn't know," I tell them both. "I had no idea."

"How?" my mother says.

"Before I left for the military, Hazel and I," I start to say, and she raises her hand to stop me from talking.

"I mean, how did you not know?" She gets up. "A father knows."

"Darlin'," my father says, grabbing her hand and pulling her down next to him.

"Hazel tried to get in touch with me," I say and swallow hard. "I ignored her."

"Hold on." My father gets up now. "Are you telling me that she said she was pregnant with your child, and you ignored her?" His voice goes loud now, and he looks like he is going to charge at me.

"No." I shake my head. "God, this is not going like I planned." I look at them. "I couldn't wait to leave here," I tell them, and I know that if I'm going to tell them about Sofia, they should know it all. "I fucking hated living here. I hated the shoes I had to fill." I brush away a tear. "Every single time I went anywhere, I was Casey Barnes son and Quinn's little brother. Every time I tried to do something, I was always compared to both of you. It ate at me, and I hated myself. I hated my life. I wanted out. I wanted to be me and only me. Reed Barnes, not Casey's son, not Quinn's brother, but just me."

"Reed," my mother says, her lower lip quivering.

"It was my living hell, and then I left. It was the best," I tell them. "I was me and no one else. When Hazel reached out to me, I felt like if I answered her, it would be me wanting to come back, so I deleted all my social media."

"Good God," my father says. "She went through all that by herself."

I nod. "Even when I saw her from afar, I didn't know. It took me meeting Sofia to put everything together." I smile now as the tears roll down my cheeks. "God, it was a love that I can't even explain. It was like my heart was going to explode in my chest. She's …" I put my hands on my hips. "She's fucking amazing, and she's mine."

"She has your smirk," my father says. "I saw it." He sits down now. "Her smile, it's …"

"What does this mean?" my mother says. "Can we be a part of her life? Can I go visit her?" She can't stop the sob. "She had the baby by herself without any help. I just can't even imagine."

"We are going to tell her today that I'm her father," I say, the smile mixing with the tears.

"Instead of Uncle Reed." My father sits down now as if all the tension has left his body. "What does that mean with your service?"

"I'm done," I say the two words that no one but my commander knew. "No way can I leave her now." I shake my head. "Not when I just got her."

My mother looks down at her hands in her lap. "This is the reason, isn't it?" my father asks, and I just look at him. "You have to know as a parent, seeing you when you got back took a piece of our souls. We would give everything we have to make sure you were happy, anything and everything." I look down, and when he looks up, I can see the anguish that it did to him. Having to go through it again, I can't even imagine how helpless they must have felt. "When you came back home, your eyes …" He stops talking now, his voice cracking. My mother grabs his hand, and they share a look. "Your eyes were dead." His eyes look at mine. "Now there is light back in them."

The tears roll down my cheeks now as I look at my parents, who would do anything in the world to make sure we are happy. My parents suffered in silence as I lived with my own demons. But looking at them and thinking about Sofia and Hazel, a smile comes to my face. I nod, looking my father in the eyes. "I guess it is, then," I say now. "They are the reason."

Twenty-Six

HAZEL

"MOMMA." I HEAR Sofia calling me, and I look over at her. "What happened to Uncle Reed?"

"What do you mean?" I ask and turn to look down at the eggs I'm making her for breakfast. I got a text from Reed this morning at seven, telling me he was on his way to his parents' house. I'm trying not to freak out about the whole thing, knowing as soon as he's done, he's going to come over here and we will tell Sofia.

"He comes for breakfast," she says, not looking up from her coloring pages. "Is he sick?"

"No," I say, placing her eggs on the plate with her two pieces of toast. "He was probably busy this morning." I put the plate down and grab my cup of coffee, knowing I'm too nervous to even bother eating. "Do you like

Uncle Reed?" I ask, bringing the cup to my mouth. I watch her nod her head. A sigh of relief comes out of me when I hear a soft knock on the door. I put my cup down and almost fly to the door.

He stands there with his head down, and my stomach sinks, thinking that they refuse to accept Sofia. The fear fills my body, turning my body cold. He looks up, and I can see he's been crying. "Hey," I say softly, my eyes searching his for the answers but coming up empty. "You okay?"

"Yeah." He nods, and I walk out of the door, going to him and hugging him. Getting on my tippy-toes, I put my arms around his shoulders. He bends just a bit, and his arms wrap around my waist. "It's okay," he whispers in my ear, and I lean back, my arms still around him. "Better than okay."

A tear falls on my arm, and I realize it's from me. Reed's hand comes up. "No tears," he says. "Not today."

"Um," I say, letting go of his shoulders. "There will be tears." I'm not even going to pretend I'll be strong enough for this. "But they will be happy tears and not sad tears."

He smirks at me, and my hand itches to come up and trace it with my finger. "I can do that."

"Uncle Reed." I feel Sofia next to me as she pushes me to the side to stand between us. "Momma didn't make you eggs."

He laughs, bending and taking her in his arms. "That's okay. I'm not hungry," he says, and I notice he's wearing shorts instead of jeans.

"Do you want coffee?" I ask over my shoulder when I walk back into the house, and he follows me. "Do you want to do this right now?" I ask, and he nods his head. My heart fills in my throat as he looks at Sofia. I ignore the way my stomach just lurched, walking over to the couch.

Reed puts down Sofia. "Come and sit for a minute." I pat the seat next to me, and she walks over to me and sits down.

"Come on, Uncle Reed," Sofia says, patting the seat next to her. He walks over, but instead of sitting next to her, he squats down in front of her.

"So remember a long time ago," I start talking. "When you asked me if you had a dad?"

I look at her to see if she remembers that morning the week after she started school when she asked me if she had a dad. She caught me off guard, and it took me a couple of minutes to answer her.

"You said he went away." She tells me my words. "But he loved me."

"I did," I say, the tears dripping off my chin. My hand goes out to hold hers. "Well …"

Reed's hand covers ours, and he speaks now for the first time. "I'm your dad," Reed says, and I look over at him and then back at Sofia.

"Why didn't you come for me?" she asks him and tilts her head to the side. "You didn't want me?" I gasp, bringing my hand to my mouth.

"I want you more than anything in the world," he says. "More than you love Caramel and tractors."

"But you didn't come to see me," she says, and I wonder if we did it at a good time. But when is it a good time to tell your child who their father is? She looks at him, not sure of anything.

"He wanted to come see you," I say. "But he was far away, and he couldn't get to you."

"The minute I could come to see you, I came," he says to her. "And I'm not going away anymore," he says. "Not now, not ever. I'll be here every single day."

"For breakfast?" she asks, and he nods. "And dinner."

He looks at me. "As long as Momma doesn't mind cooking for me."

"Momma." She looks at me. "Will you make food for Uncle Reed?"

"Of course," I say, and she looks back at Reed.

"Can we go see Caramel?" she asks him, and he nods his head.

"Yes," he says. "But, um, first, my momma and my dad want to come and meet you." My eyes open wide. "They should be here soon."

I jump up now and look down at my outfit. "I have to change." I look at Sofia. "We have to change."

Sofia must think it's a game because she starts to laugh as if it's a joke. "Let's go." I grab her hand and pick her up to move faster. "All we have are farm clothes." I look over at Reed, who has his hands on his hips.

"Well, they just got here, so …" He smiles, and I hear the sound of a door close.

"Oh my God," I say, my nerves getting the better of me. "Oh my God." I put Sofia down. "I didn't even brush my hair." I look at him, the bile in my stomach slowly rising, and I put my hand to it. "I think I'm going to be sick."

Reed walks to me now. "It's going to be fine," he says, trying to reassure me, but we didn't even talk about how they reacted to the news.

I don't have a chance to say anything because the knock on the door fills the room. "I don't even have fresh baked cookies," I whisper to Reed. The two big tears are ready to run over my eyelids.

He puts his hand on my face. "I promise you," he whispers, "it's going to be okay."

The knock comes again, and this time, Sofia pushes away from us and walks to the door. "Is it a killer?" she asks, and I close my eyes and roll my lips.

"No," I hear Casey say. "It's just Casey and Olivia."

Sofia turns back to look at us. "It's not a killer."

"I don't even know where she heard that word," I mumble under my breath as the door opens, and I see Casey standing there with Olivia beside him.

"Hi," Sofia says. "I know you," she says to Casey. "You said shit." She points at him, and Olivia gasps out and hits his arm.

"It was an accident, and I said I was sorry," he tells Olivia and then looks at Sofia. "Can we come in?"

"Okay," Sofia says, moving away from the door. "Momma didn't bake cookies." She tells them what I just said. "And Uncle Daddy Reed is my daddy," she informs them, and I close my eyes.

"And this," Reed says, going down beside her, "is my

mom and dad. Your grandma and grandpa."

Olivia kneels in front of her now. "You are the most beautiful girl in the world," she says to her, smiling through her tears. "And you have your daddy's smile." Then she holds her little hand in hers. "Can I get a little hug?"

"Okay," Sofia says, not understanding anything that is going on. She puts her arms around Olivia, who closes her eyes and cries silently. I put my hand to my own mouth, trying to stop the sobs from coming up. My girl has so much more love than she will ever know. She will never go without it for a minute in her whole life. That, to me, is everything. Reed puts his arm around me, and I turn to cry into his shoulder. "You smell good," Sofia now says. "Momma." She turns around. "She smells like a princess."

"That's because she is one." I wipe my cheeks with the palm of my hands.

"Can I get into this hug giving?" Casey says, getting down and putting his arms around her waist. "I think we need to get you fitted for some riding gear," he says. She nods her head, and I have to wonder if she even knows what he's saying.

"Momma, can I get a cookie?" She looks over at me, and I just nod as she hops over to the kitchen, not even interested in what is going on. I am a little thankful for that when I look over and see Olivia stand and come to me. Her eyes fill with tears as she walks over to me. I expect her to be angry for keeping Sofia a secret, and she has every right to be. But I can tell from the way she looks at me that she isn't angry.

"I don't even know where to start." Her voice comes out with a quiver. My insides start to shake, and I feel like my teeth are going to clatter. Reed puts his hand on my lower back. "First, I want to say thank you." Her voice cracks. "For giving us Sofia." She wipes away a tear from the corner of her eye. "There are no words I can say that will tell you what you mean to us. What you both mean to us." I blink back my tears, and she comes forward to give me the biggest hug. "Thank you for giving me my boy back," she whispers in my ear.

"Shall we sit?" Reed says, and Olivia lets me go.

"Yes," she says. "I want to get to know my grandbaby," she says, turning to Casey. "I get to take her shopping."

Reed and Casey both groan. "I'm sorry," Reed says to me. "She is going to go overboard."

"I don't know what that means." I turn to Reed again, hoping he can fill in the blanks.

"Oh, you will," Casey says, laughing and then stopping in front of me. "You gave us a gift that we can't ever repay you for," he says. I can hear the tremble of his voice and see this big man fight back his tears. "This is for you," he says, handing me the manila envelope.

My hand comes out to grab it, and I look at Reed, who just stares at it. His eyebrows pinch together while I turn the envelope over, flipping open the flap, and pull out the papers. "What is this?" I ask as my eyes scan the papers, not sure what I'm reading. My eyes are so full of tears that everything is blurry.

"That," Casey says, "is the deed to the land and the

house."

"I don't understand?" I say. "Why is my name on here?"

"Well, we wanted you to have something to come home to," he says, and Olivia just smiles. "You'll see that all debts have been paid."

I shake my head, the lump in my throat making it hard to breathe. "I ..." I start. "I can't accept this."

"It's nonnegotiable," Olivia says, standing beside Casey. "We did this," she says, and she can't come out with the words.

"What my wife is trying to say is," Casey says with a smile on his face, "welcome back home, Hazel."

Twenty-Seven

Reed

"MOMMA," SOFIA CALLS Hazel from downstairs. "Are you ready?"

"She'll be right down," I tell Sofia as she turns in a circle, wearing the new dress my mother had delivered today. "Look, Uncle Daddy," she says, and I try not to laugh at the name. "I'm like Anna from *Frozen*." I just look at her, not sure who that person is.

We both look over at the stairs as we see Hazel come down. I watch and see her feet and then her long legs. My mouth gets suddenly dry as I see more leg and finally the beige skirt. My eyes are staring at her legs as she turns, and the skirt flows around her. "I think I'm going to be sick." She puts her hand to her stomach, and I see that the white shirt she is wearing is tied at the waist.

"Momma, look," Sofia says. "I got new shoes." She goes over to pick up the new pink shoes my mother bought.

"More shoes?" Hazel asks, and I look at her and shrug. It's been two days since we told my parents Sofia was mine. Even though they wanted to go out and tell the world, we thought it would be good to tell people slowly, for Sofia's sake. At this point, I didn't give a shit who else knew because she knew I was her dad. "She got ten pairs yesterday," Hazel says, slipping her feet into the flip-flops.

"We warned you," I say, getting up from the couch. "My mother has no control when it comes to shopping. Zero. My father built her a house once, and no one went into it because she ordered all this delicate stuff, and we were afraid to ruin anything."

"What?" Hazel asks, shocked. "Wait, was that the white house?" I nod my head. "I heard about it."

"Yeah, heard about it," I say. "Never saw it." I laugh now. "I'm living in it now."

"You live in the white house?" Hazel shrieks.

"Are you the president?" Sofia looks at me. "He lives in the White House."

"I'm not the president," I say, picking her up. "Far from it. Now, let's go, or else your grandmother is going to blow up my phone again."

"Are you sure about this?" Hazel says. "I mean, babysitting."

"Hazel," I say her name. "You have to pray that she wants to come back and live with you after she's at my parents' house," I say. I don't know how my mother did it, but she called and asked to babysit Sofia for the night. I saw the turmoil in her eyes, and I said no for her, but then she caved and agreed. So tonight, we are going to drop Sofia off and then go have a drink at the bar. It's totally a date, but I'm not calling it that in front of her. I also won't admit it to her, but tonight when I drop her off, I'm taking that fucking kiss. I mean, I think I am. Fuck if I know. I've never been this nervous in my life.

"Where are the keys?" I ask Hazel, who holds up her hands. I put my hand out for them, and she looks at me.

"It's my car," she says, putting her hands on her hips.

"And I'm the man," I say, looking at Sofia. "The man always drives when you are together."

"I thought she wasn't allowed to date," Hazel reminds me, laughing as she hands me the keys. Last night, when we talked about Sofia, I said she wasn't allowed to date, something that Hazel agreed to also.

As I put Sofia in the truck, she tells me what needs to be done. She is very quick to let me know when I'm messing something up. I get into the truck and look over at Hazel, who is breathing now. "Relax." I put my hand on hers. "Worst case, my parents call us and we go get her."

"I know it's silly," she says and looks in the back. "But she's never been to a sleepover."

"Momma," Sofia says. "I have a princess bed," she tells me. "Grandma bought me one."

"Of course she did," Hazel says, shaking her head. I can't help but laugh, and when we get to my parents' house, my mother is sitting on the steps waiting. She jumps up and claps her hands.

"Cowboy!" she yells for my father. "They're here." My father comes out of the house. The minute I put the car in park, the back door springs open. "There she is," my father says. "Princess Sofia."

"See, Momma," she says. "Told you I'm a princess."

It takes about fifteen minutes for Hazel to be okay enough to walk away. After my mother shows Sofia her special room, she turns to me. "She's never coming back to Pops' house."

When we walk out of the house, I want to grab her hand when our fingers graze each other's. Sofia doesn't even come and say goodbye to us, and Hazel keeps looking out the window.

The parking lot is almost empty when we get there, which is typical for Wednesday night, but I spot my sister's truck and my cousins'. Getting out of the truck, I wait for her as we walk to the bar. "It's funny," she says, looking at me. "It's changed"—she looks around—"yet feels the same." She pulls open the door, and you can see the changes right away. "God, I used to hate this place on Saturday nights," she says, pointing at where the pool tables are. "People would spill so much shit back there."

"I know," I groan. "Who do you think used to mop it?"

"Who do you think mopped it when you left?" she counters, and I look at her. "Christopher was always 'busy.'" She makes air quotes when she says busy.

I look around and see that everyone is sitting at the

table in front of the bar. Asher sits on the stool with Amelia beside him, right next to Chelsea, sitting next to Mayson. His hand is on Chelsea's leg, just in case people don't see the ring on her finger.

"Look at what the cat dragged in," my sister says from behind the bar. Besides my parents, she is the only one who knows since she lives in the house, and my mother had to explain why she was renovating a room for a child. "What can I get you, Hazel?" She smiles at her.

"Um …" She looks at her. "Water."

"Why?" Amelia says, turning on her stool. Her stomach is sticking out. "Have a glass of wine or a shot of whiskey."

Chelsea picks up her beer and brings it to her lips. "I had to take one for the team also."

"I'll have a glass of white wine," she says and then looks at me. "I don't drink."

"Sip it," I mumble under my breath, grabbing two stools and sitting with them.

Harlow comes over and puts her wine down on a coaster and then hands me a beer. "I'll put it on your tab."

"No tab," Amelia says. "We don't know when he's going to leave town."

I laugh, picking up the beer now. "Not anytime soon," I tell them, taking a pull. "I'm out," I say, and they look at me in shock. "It was time."

"You know when you know," Mayson says, holding up his beer to me in a salute.

"What are you going to do now?" Amelia asks as she

rubs her stomach.

"I haven't decided yet," I say to them. Technically, it's the truth, but I leave out that I don't know what I'm going to do since Hazel hasn't told me what her plans are. I keep thinking that she will stay, but I'm not going to be the one to pressure her.

"Well, it's good to have you home," Amelia says and then winces. "I swear these contractions."

"They are the worst," Hazel says. "I had Braxton Hicks with Sofia for seven weeks."

"What are Braxton Hicks?" I ask, worried she was in pain for seven weeks.

"It's when you get a contraction, but it's not real," she says, but I still don't understand it. "Your body is getting ready for the real thing, so it's like a practice run."

"With Tucker, I had back pains, and I kinda knew they were contractions, but I didn't think it would go downhill so fast," Chelsea says, then looks at Mayson. "Then my water broke." Mayson's head shakes, making Chelsea laugh. "It's fine. He's healthy."

"She almost gave birth in the elevator," Mayson pipes in. "I thought I was going to die."

"You thought you were going to die?" Chelsea says. "Try squeezing a watermelon out of your …" The men groan, and I grimace and hold my junk.

"I don't know why this baby isn't coming out," Amelia says. "I've tried everything. Spicy food. Walks, raspberry tea, sex."

"Amelia," Asher says to her.

"You don't think they know we have sex?" She points

at her stomach. “Exhibit A.” It makes us all laugh.

“How was your labor?” Amelia looks at Hazel.

“It was almost sixteen hours,” she says, and the girls gasp. “After hour fourteen, I got a fever.” My mouth goes dry suddenly. “I don’t remember much after that, but it took me thirty-nine minutes to push her out.”

“Were you with the father?” Amelia asks, and Chelsea smacks her hand. “Oh my God,” she says, putting her hand to her mouth. “I’m so sorry, that was …” She holds up her hands, and I look over at Hazel, who smiles, trying to pretend it doesn’t bother her, and inside, I die just a touch. “Insensitive.”

“It’s fine,” Hazel says. “Things happen.”

“How involved is the father now?” Chelsea asks. “If you don’t want to talk about it …”

“No,” Hazel says, looking down at the wineglass in front of her that she hasn’t taken a sip from.

“It’s me,” I say, and even my brain doesn’t get what is going on. I look at my cousins, and I can see Harlow standing behind the bar with her eyes about to come out of their sockets. “I’m the father.”

Twenty-Eight

HAZEL

I WATCH THE black road, not saying anything as the words linger in my head. "I'm the father." I sat there, shocked he was coming out with it. I knew that we would start telling people since we told Casey and Olivia, but I just didn't know it would happen so fast.

"We need to tell your grandparents." I look over at him, and he nods now, his hair pushed back from his fingers.

"I mean, hopefully, they take it better than my cousins did," he says, shaking his head, and I feel so bad for him. "I thought Amelia was going to throw a glass at my head." I see him shaking his head. "If looks could kill, I would be dead right now." He looks over. "Chelsea looked at me with daggers in her eyes."

"I'm so, so sorry," I say, turning now. "I shouldn't have even answered any questions." My heart sinks.

"Why should you be sorry?" he asks, pulling into my driveway. "It's not like the truth isn't what it is."

"I know," I tell him. "But." I swallow. "I never meant to make it sound like …"

"Like I abandoned you," he says, turning the truck off and turning to look at me.

"I know that if you'd known, you would have been there," I say, and my hand goes up to open the truck door. "Thank you," I say. "For bringing me out tonight." I look down as I try to stretch the time we're together. I keep waiting for him to stop me from going in. "Have a great night," I say with a smile, and I get out before I beg him to kiss me.

I open the door and shut it just as fast without looking back to see if he is watching. All night, my senses were on alert, waiting for his touch. It started when we were walking to the bar, and our fingers grazed each other's. It continued when his leg rubbed mine. I thought I was going to pull out my hair, even with everything going on and the questions that they had for us and for me. The only thing I could concentrate on was where his leg was touching my bare leg, sending shock waves up my spine. I swear I shivered so many times I thought they were going to think I was freezing cold when, in fact, my body was on fire.

I drop my purse on the floor, kicking off my flip-flops, and make my way upstairs. "You should have asked him to stay," I tell myself. I'm about to take off my shirt when

I hear banging on the door.

I run back downstairs, my heart beating now with worry as the banging starts again. I open the door and look at Reed, who stands there with his hands holding the doorframe. He looks up at me. "Reed," I say. "Is everything okay?" I ask, wondering if maybe his mother called.

"Yeah," he says, his voice sounding like he ran a marathon. "I just forgot this." I don't even have time to think before he takes two steps to me. He puts one hand around my waist at the same time the other buries itself in my hair. "I forgot this," he whispers before his mouth crashes on mine. My hand slides up his arm and wraps around his neck as my mouth opens, and his tongue slides with mine, drowning out our moans. He kicks the door closed with his foot and picks me up now. He turns us in a circle with my back toward the door. His hand releases my hair to sit on my neck. He pushes me against the wall, our mouths playing catch-up. All those times I closed my eyes and thought about his kisses, I knew it was nothing like it would be in person. He moves his head to the other side, deepening the kiss. My hands are frantic to touch him, going to his shirt and moving it up. He only lets go of my mouth when I pull it over his head. He comes back to my mouth, his hands moving from my hips to my tits. My nipples pebble, waiting to be played with, and he pinches them through my shirt as I arch my back.

"Fuck," he says, letting go of my mouth and moving his mouth to my neck. My hands go to his belt and pull it out. "I'm sorry," he says, and my eyes open but then close again when I feel his tongue on my neck. "I wanted to be slow and romantic," he says between kisses. My eyes are closed as I feel his hands move to my hips. His hands bunch up my skirt, and when I look down, he's on his knees. "Fuck," he says again, lifting my skirt and coming face-to-face with my white thong. I feel his fingers run down my covered slit, and my whole body shivers. "I have to have a taste," he says right before I feel his fingers move my thong to the side. His tongue comes out, and he licks me, and I swear my knees feel like they'll buckle. "Open for me," he says. He lifts one of my legs over his shoulder and groans, going back in for another lick. "Sweetness." He says the same thing he said all those years ago. I try to keep my eyes open to watch him, but the feeling is just too good. His tongue slips into me, then I feel two fingers open my lips, and the tip of his tongue teases my clit. "I can't," he says as his tongue and two fingers slip into me. "Fucking go slow." I moan. One hand comes up by my head while the other one is buried in his hair. "Tell me you want it."

"I want you," I say, panting as he finger fucks me while sucking on my clit. "I want you." I repeat the words. His fingers pick up speed, and I cry out his name. "Reed," I say between pants and moans. "God," I say, moving my hips and wanting more and more.

"That's it, baby," he says right before he bites my clit. My toes curl, and I buck as my pussy pulses around his fingers when I come. "So fucking tight." He licks my clit, and his finger doesn't stop until I come down from my orgasm. He looks me in the eyes while he brings his fingers to his mouth and sucks them. My leg falls to the floor as he slides his body up. "I waited a long fucking time to do that again," he says. "And I'm going to do it again and again." His tongue licks my lower lip, my tongue coming out to find his, and I taste myself on him. "All night long," he says, "I'm going to eat you and then slide into you." His tongue comes out now to find mine. My hands go to the button of his jeans as I open them. My hand slides into his boxers as my hand fists him. "Fuck." He lets go of my lips, giving me a chance to slide down to my knees.

I pull down his boxers, the tip slipping out, and my tongue licks the precum off him. My mouth swallows the tip of his cock. He hisses out, and he pushes his pants down over his hips, giving me access to the rest of his cock. I swallow as much of him as I can, using my hand to work what I can't reach. "Hazel," he says my name over and over again as his hips move with my mouth. I let go of his cock and lick the shaft on both sides before I curl my tongue around his head. My eyes look up at him as I take his cock into my mouth again. His eyes are on mine as he fucks my mouth. I can feel him getting bigger and bigger, my hand moving at the same time, and then he steps out of my reach. I moan now, but instead, he pushes against the door. His mouth crashes on mine, and I feel him lift my skirt. He moves my panties to the side and slips in two fingers, causing my back to arch away from the door. He wraps a hand around my waist, lifting me, and his fingers slide out as he fills me with his cock.

I cry out when he pushes all the way into me, making him stop moving. "No," I groan when he doesn't move. "Don't stop." I squeeze his cock with my pussy. "Harder."

He groans out as his hands go to my hips and my legs wrap around his waist. He lifts me up and down on his cock, slamming me down each time harder and harder. He buries his face in my neck as he fucks me against the door. "Reed," I say his name as I hold on to him. "I'm …"

"Me, too," he says, his mouth covering mine again. My tongue tangles with his as he fucks me. I come first, and he swallows my moan. I can't even focus on anything else as I come over and over again. His hips lift a couple more times, and this time, he lets go of my mouth with my name on his lips in a whisper.

My hand comes up now as I touch his face. "I'm sorry. It's fucking barbaric," he says, smirking as my pussy squeezes his cock again. "You keep doing that, and we might not leave this area."

I laugh, leaning in and rubbing my nose with his. "I don't see anything wrong with that." I kiss his lips. "Just …" I say. "I'm not on the pill."

His eyes open wide. "Jesus, I didn't even think, the only thing I wanted was you," he says. "It is what it is."

"I mean, why don't we not test fate next time?" I say as his hips start moving again, the words lost now. "I mean, I did get pregnant and we used protection," I say, making him chuckle.

"What do you say?" He moves his hips again.

"I say yes," I interrupt him, and he rams into me

again. “Oh, yes.”

“What do you say we go to my house?” he says, slipping out of me. I moan, thinking he’s going to leave me in this state. “So I can have you in a bed.” He takes my shirt off now, his hand cupping my tits as he brings the cups down and takes a nipple into his mouth.

“There is a bed upstairs,” I remind him as he takes the other nipple and bites it now. “And a couch over there.”

“But Sofia sleeps in that bed,” he says. “Besides …” He turns me around, grabbing my hips and pulling me back to him so his cock rests between my ass cheeks. “My bed is bigger.” He pushes on my back, making me bend over in front of him. My hand is on the door as he lifts my hips up and slides into me again. “So after this round …” He pumps into me, his cock harder than before. “We get into the truck and finish off at my house.” One of my hands goes between my legs now. “Change of plans,” he says as the sound of flesh slapping fills the room. At this point, I’ll fucking agree to anything as long as he keeps his cock in me. “When we leave here, you suck my cock while we drive to my house.”

“Yes,” I say out in a whisper. “That sounds like a plan,” I pant out. There in the doorway, he fucks me until I agree to whatever he wants.

Twenty-Nine

REED

"IF YOU KEEP doing that …" She sticks her ass into my cock. "We are never going to leave."

"I don't know what you mean." She wiggles her ass as the shower rains over her. I think we slept thirty minutes total last night because we were so needy for one another. After doing her in her house, she did, in fact, suck my cock as I drove home. It's a good thing it was the middle of the night because it took me five minutes, and I had to stop in the middle of the road a couple of times. The minute I put the car in park, she threw her leg over me and sank down on my cock. I finally got her in the bed for round five and fucked her with her arms and legs around me. The covers were thrown on the floor, the pillows on the side tables as my girl gave it to me as good as I gave it to her. She drops the soap on the floor and bends fully, something she's done a couple of times already. "Oops." She opens her legs, and it takes me one second to think about it before I bend my knees and slip into her. "Okay, one more time," she says. I grab her hips and turn to sit on the bench in the shower.

Taking her with me, I thrust my cock deeper and deeper into her. I take her legs and put them on top of mine as she starts to move. Her head drops onto my shoulder as she turns her mouth for my tongue. One of my hands goes to her clit while the other tweaks her nipple. Her pussy grips me tight, and I know she loves it. "I'm there," she says, her hand coming to play with mine at her clit. "Right there," she says, and I know once she comes, she will stop moving.

She screams out as she comes, and I'm not wrong. She stops moving. "You done?" I ask, and she nods.

"You want my mouth?" she asks with a twinkle in her eyes as she slips off me, and her mouth swallows me. It doesn't take long before I come down her throat.

"You ruined me," I say as she gets up and starts to wash herself off. "And if we didn't have to be at my parents' house, I'd have you ride my face."

She splashes water at me. "You can't tease me like that," she says. "You know I love your mouth."

I get up and kiss her mouth. "Oh, I know," I say, walking out of the shower. I grab a towel and hold out one for her when she steps out of the shower.

"I have to go to my house," she says as she dries herself off. That first night in the barn, I knew she was stunning, but when I see her in the light, her beauty always stops me in my tracks. She is even more beautiful than before.

"Well, you tore my panties in the car," she reminds me. "And my shirt is ripped right down the middle."

"Hey"—I point at her—"I asked if you minded."

"You had two fingers in me." She laughs. "I would have agreed to anything."

"Good to know." I wink at her and slap her ass, and instead of saying ouch, she just moans. My cock twitches. "Really good to know."

She puts on my T-shirt and shorts and we drive to her house. My hand rests on her leg as we get to her house. My phone rings, and I see it's my mother. "Hello," I answer on speaker.

"Daddy Uncle Reed," Sofia says softly. "Are you coming to get me? I miss Momma."

"We are going to be there in five minutes," I say, and if I knew that Hazel wouldn't freak out, I would drive there now with her wearing my clothes. "How about we go ride Caramel?"

"Yes," she says, and I can picture her smile. "Grandma, I'm going to ride Caramel."

"Okay, baby, let me talk to Daddy." She hands her the phone. "Sorry, I tried to stall her, but …"

"It's fine. We just got back to Hazel's. She's going to change, and we'll be right there." Hazel gasps and slaps me, and I look over at her as her eyes go big.

"Oh, no need. Your father is going to your grandparents' right now. He'll take her riding while you talk to your grandfather," she tells me.

"So you heard?" I ask, and she hums.

"Harlow gave us the rundown," she says. "Amelia said you have until noon, and then she's going to tattle."

"Thanks, Mom," I say, hanging up.

"Seriously?" Hazel says. "Seriously, you had to tell her we spent the night together."

"Well, considering you're spending the night with me again tonight, she's going to know," I say as she gets out and storms up the steps.

"Oh, no, I'm not," she says over her shoulder.

"You sure about that?" I ask, leaning against the truck. "Hurry up, my daughter is sad."

She slams the door in my face, and it takes everything not to chase after her and turn her ass red. She comes out in record time wearing tight pink jeans with a black T-shirt tucked into the front. "How do I look?" she asks.

"Good enough to eat." She stops in front of me, and I pull her to me. "I missed you," I say softly, and she puts her hands around my shoulders. "Give me a kiss," I say, and I can see she wants to fight with me. "Please."

She smirks. "Better," she says, and she kisses me. I open the door for her, and I admit if she lets me do this with her for the rest of her life, I'm going to die a happy man.

I get into the truck and make my way over to my grandparents' house. "I don't know about this," she says, putting a hand to her stomach. "Why don't you tell him and then call me?"

I'm about to argue with her when the front door opens and my grandmother comes out. "Too late." I get out of the truck, and when she gets out of the truck, she glares at me. "Can I hold your hand?"

"I will not give you my mouth for a month," she says through clenched teeth, making me laugh as I shake my head.

"Well, look at you two," my grandmother says. "Thick as thieves with those secrets."

I laugh now and kiss her cheek. "Where is Grandpa?" I ask as she holds out her arms for Hazel.

"He's finishing lunch," she says. "Come on in. Did you guys eat?"

"Yeah," I say, walking in behind her. "I ate a couple of times today. I ate a ton last night," I say over my shoulder, and if my grandmother wasn't watching, she would have kicked me in the ass.

"Billy," my grandmother says. "Look who came."

He looks up and smiles when he sees me. His smile grows bigger when he sees Hazel. "Isn't that a sight for sore eyes?"

"Hi, Mr. Barnes," Hazel says.

"Sit down, please," my grandmother says. "Can I get you two something to drink?"

"I'm fine," Hazel says. I pull out a chair for her, and my grandmother watches, her eyes narrowing. She used to give me the same look when she would tell me that she would tan my hide if I messed up her flowers with my soccer ball.

"Come and sit," I tell my grandmother, and she comes over, knowing that something is coming. She sits next to Grandpa as they share a look. "We came over today …"

I start to say.

"We?" My grandfather picks up. "There is a we?"

I reach across the table and grab Hazel's hand as she has tears in her eyes. I'm sure she's a nervous wreck. "There is a we," I tell them, smiling now and feeling so proud. "In more ways than just the two of us."

"I don't understand," my grandmother says, and then she puts her hands in front of her mouth. "Reed Barnes, is she pregnant?"

I don't say she might be because we definitely were not careful, like at all. "No." I shake my head. "But she was."

My grandmother starts to cry. "You are such an idiot," Hazel says under her breath.

"Mr. and Mrs. Barnes, what he's trying to say and failing so miserably at is that Sofia," she starts to say and then stops, and I see she won't be able to continue.

"Sofia is my daughter," I finally say, and my grandmother's hand comes down from her mouth now, but her mouth does not close.

"What?" my grandfather whispers as he looks at me.

"I found out I was pregnant right before I left," Hazel says. "Pops …"

"He knew, didn't he?" Grandpa asks. "He knew Reed was the father?"

"He did," she says, and I can see her lips tremble, so I pull her chair to me. "But I made him promise not to tell you," she says. "I didn't want to be a burden."

"Be a burden?" my grandmother says. "You gave us a gift. A child is a gift," she says, grabbing a tissue. "Why didn't you tell us?" She looks at me.

"She tried to tell me, and I fucked up," I admit. "I fucked up so bad."

"Pops," my grandfather says, grabbing the handkerchief that he keeps in his shirt pocket. "Every single time he went out to see you," he says, his voice trembling as he thinks about his friend. "He would come over here and show us all of his pictures," he says, looking at my grandmother. "All he could say was isn't she a beauty, Billy." Hazel puts a hand to her mouth now. "He was sharing her with us without us knowing." My grandfather stops talking now as he composes himself. "That sneaky son of a bitch," he says, laughing. "He was a good man."

"He was," Hazel says. "And he thought the world of you."

"We have another great-granddaughter," my grandfather says to my grandmother, who just nods her head.

"The more, the merrier," she says. "You did an amazing job, Hazel." She looks at her, and I grab Hazel and bring her forehead to mine.

The back door opens and my father is carrying Sofia in his arms. "See, I told you they were here." She squirms out of his arms.

"Momma," she says, going to Hazel and getting into her lap and hugging her.

Hazel wraps her arms around her. "I missed you." She kisses her head. "What are you wearing?" She looks down at Sofia's outfit.

"These are horse pants," she says.

"Riding pants," my father says. "Your mother." I hold my hand up like I get it. "Is everything okay here?" my father asks, and I know he came in to have my back.

"Everything is great," my grandfather says. "We were just catching up." He looks over at my father, who nods his head.

"Yeah," I say, smiling with Sofia and Hazel beside me, and a sense of peace comes over me. "Everything is great."

Thirty

HAZEL

“DON’T TOUCH THAT,” I snap when I see Sofia walking to the little coffee table and picking up what can only be described as a vase or maybe a bowl. Whatever it is, I’m sure it costs more money than I care to think of.

“She can touch anything she wants,” Reed says, coming out from the bedroom. “Everything can be replaced.” His hair is wet from the shower. It’s been two days since the cat has been out of the bag with everyone. “Hi,” he says, coming to me now as I pour myself some coffee. His hands go to my hips, and he bends his head to kiss my neck. “My shower isn’t the same without you.”

“Well, did you want to explain to Sofia why we were both in the shower, and you have that”—I point at his dick—“and not a vagina like her?”

"She asked me yesterday when she climbed into bed with us." He shakes his head as I hand him his cup. "She thought it was a sword."

I step closer to him. "It kind of is." I wink at him and tilt my head back so he can kiss me. I didn't know it could be like this. Before, when we were together, it always happened at night, so no one really knew. Now he holds my hand whenever we walk out of the house, and he hugs me just as much, and don't get me started with the affection. He wraps one hand around my waist and pulls me to him.

"I think Sofia needs another sleepover at Grandma's," he says, and I laugh.

"Three times a week is enough." I bring the cup to my mouth, smirking.

The front door opens, and I'm about to step back from him. He must sense it, but he keeps me close to him. "Good morning." I hear Quinn and then see him walking into the big open area that is the family room and kitchen. "Oh, good, at least you're dressed," he says and looks at Sofia.

"How's my favorite niece?" he says, and she smiles at him. He picks her up and throws her in the air, and she giggles. "Who's your favorite uncle?" he asks, blowing kisses into her neck.

When we told his grandparents, the next stop was Quinn's place. Reed wanted to be the one to tell him. He was the most supportive out of all. He put an arm around him and said he was happy to have his brother back. He didn't care how he got here, but that he was here.

"She's your only niece," Reed says to him. "By the way, how did you get in?"

"The door was open," he says, putting Sofia down and coming into the kitchen now.

"What if Hazel was naked?" he asks, and I gasp out and push away from him.

"I don't sleep naked, nor do I walk around the house naked," I say. Walking over to the cabinet, I take out another coffee mug and fill it for Quinn.

"She's lying," Reed says, and I glare at him. "But seriously," he says, "what are you doing here?"

"I'm here to see if my girl wants to come to the barn with me," he says loud enough for Sofia to hear. "I was going to go on a ride and thought who do I know who likes to ride horses."

"Me," Sofia says, jumping now. "It's me."

"How about we eat something, and then we can go," Reed says. "You want to come with us?" He looks at me, and I shake my head.

"I have an appointment at nine," I say, walking to the fridge and opening it. "Is it pancakes or eggs?" I look over at Sofia, who yells for pancakes. "Are you staying?" I ask Quinn, who smirks.

"Will you put blueberry and lemon in them?" He mentions the pancakes I made yesterday, and I smile.

"If you come back tomorrow, I'll make the brown sugar spice ones," I say.

"Go home," Reed says. "And don't come back." I laugh as I start making the pancakes. I feel him behind me now.

"What are you doing?" I ask over my shoulder and feel him hug me.

"I'm getting my sugar," he says, and I laugh and kiss his lips.

"Go dress Sofia, and I'll cook breakfast," I say and then roll my lips. "But wait until your sword goes down."

He throws his head back and laughs. It takes him a good five minutes before he walks away, and I already have the first batch on the griddle. They polish off the twelve pancakes I make, leaving one for me and one for Sofia.

"Okay, give your momma a kiss," Quinn says, pushing away from the table and taking his plate over to the sink. "Thank you for breakfast," he says.

Sofia jumps from her chair, coming over to me. "Bye, Momma." She puckers her lips for mine.

I push her hair away from her face, and her eyes are filled with happiness. "I love you, baby girl," I say. "To the moon."

"And back." She finishes the sentence for me. "Favorite Uncle Quinn," she says, running, as I laugh and Reed groans.

"He taught her that," he says, getting up now and bringing his own plate to the sink. "Ass," he says, coming to me and leaning down. I smile and bring my hand up to his face. "See you later, baby," he says softly and kisses me with just as much softness. "Love you," he says, and we both just stop moving. My mouth runs dry, and I look at Reed, who looks like he wants the floor to open up and swallow him. "See you later," he says, turning and practically running out of the house.

My eyes blink slowly as I hear his voice again in my head, *love you.* I get up, picking up my phone, and see I have thirty minutes to get to my meeting. I walk out of the house wearing the yellow sundress I had from high school. It's a bit tighter across the top, but other than that, it fits. I lock the truck door and walk across the street toward the shop.

When I walk in, I stop in my tracks. "Oh my," I say, looking around. She did not mess around. The last time I was here, it was an empty space. Now there is a long wooden counter and a big

glass display case at the back of the store.

The walls look like the inside of a barn, and toward the back are two brown barn doors that open to the kitchen. "Hey," Savannah says, coming out from the back with a smile on her face as big as I've ever seen. "Just in time. They just installed the ovens. Come and take a look." She motions with her head, and I walk into the back. A big stainless steel island sits in the middle of the room, and then two ovens are on one wall, and two more are on the other. Muffin pans and cake pans are all stacked on a shelf.

"This …" I turn, taking it all in. "This is incredible."

"I did get a little help from Olivia with my vision." She folds her arms. "But this really did turn out amazing."

My heart beats in my chest as I think of the words to say. "I was wondering," I start to say, and then I put my hand to my stomach when I feel it lurch. "I was wondering if the offer was still on the table." I finally say the words I've been holding back for the past two days. I knew the day we told his grandparents that I wasn't leaving to go back home. The minute he told me about Pops, I knew that the best thing for Sofia would be to stay here, surrounded by family and people who love her.

"Are you joking?" she asks, and I blink away the big tears.

"No," I say. "But if we are going to be partners, it's going to be fifty-fifty." My hand comes up to wipe away the tear. "I'm going back home next week to pack up our stuff and put my condo up for sale. The prices have doubled since I bought it, so I should have enough." I take a deep breath. "I also have some savings and a nice-size retirement cushion."

"If you think," she says, "that I'm going to let you touch your retirement, you have lost your damn mind. Why don't we talk numbers tomorrow?" she says. "For today, let's talk about plans."

"I can't believe I'm going to do this," I say, looking around. "I've never imagined being a business owner before." I smile shyly. "Half business owner."

"Well, I can tell you it's a pretty big accomplishment," she says. "Now, look at these."

She grabs the stack of papers, and by the time I look up, it's already after three in the afternoon. "Wow," Savannah says. "We pretty much did all the paperwork, and I didn't hate it." She laughs.

"Thank you," I say. "For the opportunity." She comes over to me and gives me a huge hug.

"Thank you," she says softly, "for having faith in me."

I walk out of the shop with a swing in my step. I arrive back at Pops' house to find it empty. Picking up the phone, I call Reed, who answers me right away. "Where have you been?" he says. "You haven't called me all day."

"I …" I start to say. "Where are you guys?"

"At the barn," he says, and I hear water in the back. "We are giving Caramel a bath."

"I'll be right there," I say, rushing out of the house, and when I pull up to the barn, I see them at the side of the barn in the little closed area on the concrete. Reed is behind Sofia as she sprays the water on Caramel. His shirt is off, and he's wearing big rain boots.

"You always start at the feet," he says. "Like that, you don't scare her, and then you go up slowly." I don't move because all I can do is watch her with him. From the minute he found out Sofia was his, he was all in. He didn't blink an eye, didn't tell me it couldn't be. He wasn't in my face about a DNA test. I mean, even if he did, I have been with one man my whole life, and that's him. "Nice and slow," he says, guiding her hand with the water as he moves up. She listens to every single word he says, and when he hands her the glove and picks her up, he tells her how to wash the horse. "Look at how amazing you are." He kisses her neck. "You can do anything. You know that, baby girl?"

"I know," Sofia says.

"He's good with her." I jump when I hear a man's voice and turn to see Casey coming to stand with me. "I didn't mean to scare you," he says, stopping beside me. "I never thought I would see the day," he says. "To be honest, I never thought he would come back home." I smile at him. "You saved him," he says, his voice choking. "He was dead inside and didn't even know it, but you," he says, wiping the tears from his eyes, "and that little girl made him live again."

"I don't think it was all us," I say, not wanting him to feel bad.

He laughs and shakes his head. "Watching him every single day with her is like him seeing life from her eyes. It's like he's reliving his childhood, and for the first time, he isn't angry about it." He puts his arm around my shoulders. "That's all you." Reed must feel our eyes on him because he looks over and smiles, waving his hand in the air at us. "As a parent, it doesn't get better than this." He drops his hand now and walks toward them, watching Sofia giggle when he calls her Caramel Sunshine. I know that the decision I've made to stay here is the right one. I just hope Reed also thinks so.

Thirty-One

Reed

"DO YOU WANT to go and put her to bed?" Hazel asks as she gets up from the table and takes the plates away. "She looks like she's already half asleep." She motions with her head toward Sofia, who holds her head up with her hand.

"Yeah," I say, looking over at Hazel, who has been quiet all night long. Actually, she was silent all day long.

"Do you need me to help you clean up?" I ask, and she just shakes her head, her eyes not even meeting mine.

"I'm fine," she says nonchalantly.

"Okay, my girl," I say to Sofia, clapping my hands together. "Time for a bath and bed."

I hold out my hands. "Okay, Daddy," she says, and her eyes can barely stay open. She stopped calling me Uncle

Daddy Reed and then just went with Daddy. I swear to God I thought my knees would give out, and I would fall into a heaping mess while I sobbed like a baby.

I walk with her to the guest bathroom. "Bath or shower?" I ask as she puts her head on my shoulder. "How about we do a nice hot bath?" I say. "And then you can climb right into bed."

Turning on the water, I set her on the toilet, and her head falls forward. "Dad, do I have to take a bath?"

I peel off her socks, and dust comes out of them. "Yes," I say and stand her up. The bath is as fast as I can go, and when I tuck her into bed, she's asleep before I walk out of the room. I leave the door ajar and turn on the night-light I put in the hallway for her.

When I walk back into the kitchen, it's spotless and very, very empty. I look around and then find her sitting outside on the back porch. "Hey," I say, pushing open the door. "I was looking for you."

She looks over her shoulder. "Just watching the stars." She looks up. "Is she sleeping?"

"Out before I even left the room," I say, sitting next to her. I look down at my hands. If it was last night, I would have put my arm over her shoulder and pulled her to me. But today, telling her I love you was a mistake. Not that I regret telling her, but that maybe she wasn't ready to hear it.

"I have to tell you something," she says softly, and I can feel her pulling away from me. My heart is starting to beat erratically as the thought of losing her becomes so much more real.

"No," I say, my tone coming out a bit harder than I want it to. "Before you say anything." I look at her. My heart yearns to touch her, but I'm not sure she'll let me. This woman, who didn't hold any grudges toward me for bailing on her when she needed me. This woman, who, without a doubt, saved my fucking soul when I was drowning, yet I didn't even know. "I'm sorry about this morning."

"What happened this morning?" she asks, confused.

"I told you I love you." I repeat the words.

"So you don't love me?" Her eyes fill with tears, and the torture of seeing her in pain is too much to bear.

"Of course I love you," I say. "God, I love you so much, but I know you aren't there yet." She holds her hand up to talk, but I shake my head. "I know it's too soon. I know we just got back together and you probably aren't ready for it. I mean, we weren't really together before." My own tears come to my eyes now. "I want to remind you of what I said before. I'll go wherever you go, whenever. I don't care as long as you two are there."

She puts her palm on my cheek. Her touch calms my nerves. I turn my head and kiss the palm of her hand. "Is that so?" she asks with a little smirk. "What if I told you that I've decided to stay here?"

"What?" I whisper.

"Being here with Sofia and seeing her flourish with all the love she has around her." I reach out to wipe a tear rolling down her cheek. "It would be crazy. Her not knowing what it's like to grow up surrounded by her cousins. Her not knowing what Sunday really stands for. Everything I thought I wanted to run away from is exactly what I want to teach Sofia." She lowers her eyes. "I'm going to open a business," she says, her eyes lighting up, "with Savannah in town. A little coffee and bakery shop."

"How?" I ask, shocked now.

"She came to see me a couple of weeks ago, and I turned her down," she says. "But then everything just fell into place, and I knew I couldn't leave here. I know you always hated it here, and I was hoping you would maybe think of staying. But if you absolutely say you can't, we can leave."

"Where would we live?" I ask, wondering if she had all these plans. I also want to tell her that I'll fucking live in a barn as long as she's there.

"We can live at Pops' house." She cuts in now. "I know it's smaller than this house."

"If you want to live at Pops' house, we are going to have to renovate," I say. "That's nonnegotiable."

"We can do that," she says. "But it does have two bedrooms."

"Exactly," I say. "I don't just want to live here with you. I want to grow a family with you. I want to have more babies with you."

"Is that so?" She laughs, and I lean in and kiss her lips.

"We made a pretty amazing one without even trying. Can you imagine if we put some effort into it?" I smirk at her, and she throws her head back and laughs. "So yeah, I want to have more babies." And I wait to break the next news to her. "The house needs to be knocked down and rebuilt."

"It's not that bad," she says, rolling her eyes.

"I can't even stand in that shower. I would have to put my head to the side," I joke with her.

"Fine," she huffs out. "We can add another bathroom."

"And family room," I add. "And playroom."

"Okay, okay." She puts her hands up. "It's not ideal."

"That's my girl," I say. Putting my arm around her, I pull her to me and hug her.

"Reed." She says my name as she buries her face in my neck.

"Yeah, baby." My cheek rubs her head.

"I love you, too." She pulls her head out of my neck, and my gaze meets hers. "I was going to tell you this morning, but you ran out of the house like your tail was on fire."

"I didn't run out of the house." It's my turn to roll my eyes. "I left." She laughs as she kisses my lips. "In a hurry."

"Okay," she says. "Whatever you say."

I stand and hold my hand out to her. "Let's go to bed," I say, and she looks at her watch.

"It's six thirty," she says, laughing.

"Well, I haven't had dessert," I say. "And then I want to make love to you and hope I put a baby in you."

She puts her hand into mine. "Well, when you say it like that." She laughs, and I pick her up as she squeals with laughter.

I carry her to bed, where I make love to her over and over again while I thank her over and over again for giving me everything I didn't know I needed.

Epilogue One

Hazel

One month later

"THAT IS THE last box," Reed says, carrying in the last box from the truck and bringing it over to the side where all the other boxes are. "Told you it wasn't going to be as bad as you thought."

I put my hands on my hips. "That's because I thought we would have to move everything." I look around the house, seeing the boxes everywhere. "How was I supposed to know it would be furnished?" When I put the condo on the market, I had no idea that there would be not only an offer but a bidding war within forty-eight hours.

"We could have always kept the condo and used it as

our vacation home," he says, walking to the fridge now and grabbing a bottle of water. I watch him lean back against the white counter, his jeans and shirt dusty from unloading the truck that got here a couple of hours ago.

I put my hands on my hips. "A vacation home." I shake my head. "Sofia didn't even want to come with us to pack the condo. She said bring home my stuff." The minute I mentioned I was going back to our place, she got really quiet and thought we were leaving the farm. It cemented that my decision to move back home was the right one. I never thought she would like country life, but she has flourished. It was like she was born there. "If it's up to her, she'll never leave the farm."

The door flies open, and I look over to see Sofia running in with her Rubber boots. "Momma, Grandpa Casey bought me a tractor, and it's pink," she says, wiping her hair from her face. I look down at her and then look up again to see Casey coming in with papers in his hand.

"Did you actually buy her a pink tractor?" I ask even though I know he probably did.

"She said please," he counters, and I look at Reed, who just shakes his head. "I'm here for two things," Casey says. "One to ask if Sofia can come with us fishing tomorrow?" I look at Sofia, who jumps up and down.

"Can I?" she asks over and over as she jumps. The smile on her face is so big I couldn't say no if I wanted to.

"What is number two?" Reed asks.

"Here is the deed to the house," he says, holding up

the papers. "Officially yours."

"What's officially yours?" I ask, confused. "What house?" I look at Reed, who knows exactly what his father is talking about but avoids my eyes.

"This house," Casey says of the white house we've been living in. We agreed to renovate Pops' house, but when the inspector came in, he found a crack in the foundation and termite damage. The only way to fix it was to demolish it. I spent the day cleaning out his room with Reed by my side. He made me see that Pops didn't care about the house. He cared that I was here.

"Why?" I ask, looking back at Reed, who still pretends he's inspecting the ceiling all of a sudden. "Why would you give us the deed to the house?"

"It's on his work contract," Casey says, pointing at Reed. "Quinn got it when he took over his part of the farm, and now that Reed is taking over my part of the farm, he gets the house."

"What job gives you a house?" I shake my head.

"You can either take it now or take it when I die," Casey says, and I have to roll my eyes. What is it with everyone and dying?

"I don't want you to die," Sofia says, walking to Casey. "Can you not die?"

He picks her up. "I'm not going anywhere." He kisses her neck. "Now, do you want to go and see Grandma Olivia? I heard she bought someone some nail polish."

She squeals now. "Momma, I'm going now." She squirms out of Casey's arms and runs over to me, hugging me, and then runs to Reed. "Dad, I'm going to glamify."

"Glamify," I repeat and look over at Casey.

"She did not learn that from me," he says and holds her hand while he walks out. The door slams, and I turn to glare at Reed.

"I think you forgot to mention that you got a house with your job." I fold my arms over my chest, and he smirks at me.

"Must have slipped my mind." He walks over to me and takes my hand, leading us to the bedroom.

"What are you doing?" I ask as he walks past the bed and to the bathroom.

"I need to take a shower," he says, letting go of my hand and walking over to the shower to turn the water on. "And I need you to wash my back."

He pulls off his shirt and reaches for my shirt, pulling it over my head. His mouth goes to my nipple. I hiss when he sucks it, and he looks at me. "I think I'm getting my period," I say. "They are really sensitive." I blink now and look at him as I think back to when I had my period last. "Oh, no," I say, turning and running out of the room. "Did I have it when I got here?" I ask myself, and then I think I had it for sure when I got here because we had to leave the house and then rush out to get them. "Phew." I think, turning on my phone.

"Can I know what is going on?" I hear Reed from behind me.

"My period," I start to say, looking at the dates. "When was the last time I got it?"

"Well, we've been here a month, and there are no feminine products," he tells me. "Unless you keep them hidden."

I look at him. "Why would I hide them?" I ask, annoyed. "It's been seven weeks." I put my hand to my stomach and sit down, the tears starting to come now. "I wasn't even paying attention between moving here and opening the store." Which is the best thing I could have ever done. Every single day we sell out, the place is jam-packed, and we have even had some interest in doing a paint night once a week. "And all of this."

"What are you saying right now?" he says, his own face almost falling. "Are you saying you could …"

"I mean"—I close my eyes—"we have sex once a day."

He pffts out. "You mean two or three." He puffs out his chest.

"Relax, Romeo, there is no one here, so no need to whip it out." I look at the ceiling now. "What the …" I close my eyes now. "I can't believe this." I mean, we were never ever careful, not one time. Who gets pregnant this fast? I look down at my hands. I look over and see that Reed has left. "Reed." I call his name, and then he walks back into the room, his shirt now on.

"Only one way to find out," he says, holding out his hand to me. "Let's go get some tests."

"How are you not freaking out right now?" I ask, and he comes over to me, pulling me up.

"Because together everything is going to be okay." He kisses me, and I nod. "Oh, fuck," he says, turning and running back to the bedroom. He comes out now. "I might as well do this now," he says. "And if I do it after the test, you are going to spin it in your head that it's for a completely different reason." He starts mumbling, and I look at him, confused.

Until he gets down on one knee. "Reed Billy Barnes," I say his full name. "I will gut you like a fish if you don't get up."

He smirks now and looks down at the brown box in his hand. "I had this whole thing set up, but …" He smiles now. "But just like us, we like to do things just a touch backward." I put my hands to my mouth now. "I've loved you since I was eighteen years old." His voice dips. "For six years, you were locked in a box, and I knew if I opened it up, I knew that it would be the same all over again." The tears stream down my face now. "You opened that door, and it was as if I could breathe again. It was as if I had died six years ago, and I was now coming to life."

I put my hands on his cheeks, kissing his lips. "Reed," I whisper.

"You gave me our little girl," he continues. "There is no one I would think of living this life with besides you. Hazel"—he opens the box—"will you marry me?"

"Reed," I say, getting on my knees in front of him and burying my face in his neck.

He hugs me in his arms. "Is that a no?" I can hear the humor in his voice, and the only thing I can do is say one word.

"Yes." I close my eyes as my tears fall. He peels me away from him and slips on the ring that was in the box. I look down and see the huge round diamond and the pink gold with little diamonds all the way around.

"This ring is huge," I say, looking at him.

"Sofia picked it out," he says. "This was the smallest one she picked out," he says, getting up, and all I can do is look at the ring. He walks me out of the house, putting me in the truck, and when we get out, I walk in and buy fifteen tests.

"Um, shouldn't one be enough?" he asks when we get back home, and I look at him.

"No, because if one is not sure, you have a backup," I say, opening the boxes.

He picks up one box. "This says two lines is positive, and this one tells you yes or no," he reads. "How are you going to do this? Just pee in a cup and stick them all in like they are stir sticks?" I look at him, thinking that might not be a bad idea. "Go pee in the cup, and I'll get the stir sticks ready."

"Um …" I shake my head. "You aren't going to touch my pee," I say, and he laughs.

"It's just pee," he says. I grab two sticks, walk into the bathroom, and he follows me.

"Stay here," I say when I close the door. "I'm going to pee on these two, and if anything, we can do two more later." I pull down my pants and grab the two sticks, holding them together.

I place them on the counter and flush. "Can I come in now?" he asks, opening the door.

"Three minutes," I say, walking out of the bathroom and pushing him out with me. "We wait three minutes."

"Should we watch them?" He points at the tests.

"They're not a cake. You don't watch them. You sit down and wait for three minutes, and it's going to feel like it's eighty-four years," I say, sitting on the bed.

"I don't know if I can wait three minutes," he says. "It's been, what, a minute so far?"

I laugh. "It's been ten seconds."

"This will be better if I watch them," he says, walking into the bathroom.

"I'm staying here," I say, and my legs start to move now. "If this is negative, we are having safe sex until we are ready," I inform him. "No more playing Russian roulette with my ovaries." I tilt my head to look into the bathroom and see him examining the sticks. "What do they say?"

"It's not time yet," he says and picks the other one up. "But"—he looks at me—"one says yes, and the other has two lines." I get up now. "Will they change?"

"I don't know," I say, standing next to him, picking up one. "We should do another one."

Thirty minutes later, another five tests have come back positive. "Well," Reed says, then looks at me. "Do you think it's another girl?" I put my head back and groan, closing my eyes before he finally takes me in the shower.

Nine months later, our baby boy blesses us.

Epilogue Two

REED

Seven years later

"I THINK HE'S out," I say, walking out of our son's room and looking over to see that it's seven o'clock.

"Did he whine?" Hazel asks, walking to the fridge, her hair wet from the shower. "He usually likes to nurse to go to sleep." In the past seven years, I've fallen more and more in love with my wife. I put a matching wedding band on her finger the week after we found out we were having a boy. With Sofia in the middle of us, we said our vows, and it's been blissful ever since.

"In one month, he's already taken over everything," I say, sitting down on the stool with my head hanging. "Why is it so much harder than Kaine?"

"Maybe because he knows we aren't having another child, so he's going to make sure we stick to our guns." I laugh, thinking of our son Denver. He came into the world with a roar and never stopped. He came out with his nights and days screwed up, and we just got him figured out, but now he's decided that sleep, in general, is overrated.

The front door opens, and we both look over to see our thirteen-year-old daughter coming into the house. She has grown up to be even more beautiful than I can explain, making being a father to a girl so much harder. "Is he finally sleeping?" She stops, and Harlow also stops behind her.

"Should we even be talking?" Harlow asks, looking around. "I don't want to wake him."

"He should be out for at least an hour," Hazel says, closing her eyes. "I fucking hope."

Harlow laughs now. "Okay, kiddo," she tells Sofia. "Give me a hug. I'll be gone this weekend."

Sofia walks to her and gives her a hug, turning and walking to her room on her tippy-toes.

"Are you really going to that wedding?" I look at her as she walks to the kitchen.

"What am I supposed to do?" She sits down next to me. "I made a promise, and a promise is a promise."

"I don't think you need to keep a promise you made to an ex-boyfriend," Hazel says. "An ex-boyfriend you still love."

She rolls her eyes at Hazel. "I don't still love him. Besides, I got an invitation. If I don't show up, he's going to know it bothers me." She pushes off the counter. "I'll go to the wedding, show my face, smile, and wish him well." She shows us the smile she'll use. "See? Fine." She turns on her heels and storms out of the house.

"This is not going to be good," Hazel says.

"You can say that again." I shake my head. "Nothing about that was good." I get up and walk over to her, kissing her on her neck.

"He's not going to know what hit him," Hazel says. "What do you say we go and nap?"

I grab her hand and head to our bedroom. "That has to be the sexiest thing you've ever said to me."

I'm about to fall onto the bed when I hear the grunting of our son. "Oh, look, our little ray of sunshine is up," Hazel says, making me laugh.

She's helped make me whole. She's helped me be the best man I can be. Seven years ago, I thought I had it all until I saw what I was missing. "Love you," I say for the hundredth time just today.

"Love you more." She smiles. "Forever."

Are you ready for The Southern Wedding Series?

Harlow

I promised him I would be there for the best day of his life.
Not thinking I wouldn't be the one standing next to him.
But here I was attending the love of my life's wedding day.
I smiled when I saw him and pushed back the tears that wanted to come out.
This was his day and I was going to fulfill my promise.

Travis

It was supposed to be the best day of my life.
But the second I got up, things started to fall apart.
Caterer cancelled.
Flowers were from a funeral.
My bride-to-be just had an allergic reaction leaving by ambulance.
Oh and my ex-girlfriend just walked in the church.
They say you have to see the signs when they are right in front of you.
Maybe she was just mine to have.

Made in the USA
Columbia, SC
14 September 2021